For Jim,

my dearest friend and severest critic . . .
who made me follow this journey to its end.

WORLD'S END

WORLD'S END

JOAN D. VINGE

TOR

A Tom Doherty Associates Book
New York

WORLD'S END

Copyright © 1984 by Joan D. Vinge

A Tor Book
Published by Tom Doherty Associates
175 Fifth Avenue
New York, NY 10010

www.tor-forge.com

Tor® is a registered trademark of Macmillan Publishing Group, LLC.

The Library of Congress Cataloging-in-Publication Data is available upon request.

ISBN 978-0-7653-8178-1 (trade paperback)

Our books may be purchased in bulk for promotional, educational, or business use. Please contact your local bookseller or the Macmillan Corporate and Premium Sales Department at 1-800-221-7945, extension 5442, or by email at MacmillanSpecialMarkets@macmillan.com.

First Edition: November 1984
First Trade Paperback Edition: December 2017

Printed in the United States of America

0 9 8 7 6 5 4 3 2 1

The mind of man is capable of anything—because everything is in it, all the past as well as all the future.

—Joseph Conrad, *Heart of Darkness*

Nothing of him that doth fade
But doth suffer a sea-change
Into something rich and strange.

—William Shakespeare, *The Tempest*

"Shall I bring the prisoners to your office, Inspector?" the voice from his desk speaker asked him.

And again, when he didn't answer, "Inspector Gundhalinu?"

Gundhalinu turned away from the high window at last, from the view of Foursgate shrouded in mist, the rococo pattern of rain tracks on the glass. He had been looking at the Pantheon; it was just visible from where his office lay, its multiple domes of azure and gold ceramic half obscured by newer, more graceful structures. He took an antique watch from his pocket, glancing absently at the time . . . looking at the watch itself, turning it over and over for the feel of its comfortable familiarity in his hand. He sighed. The hour was getting late—but not late enough that he could postpone this final duty for another day.

Besides, he had no more days left. The ceremonies at the Pantheon were due to begin today at sunset, and they would drag on through half of tomorrow. Crowds were gathering there already . . . gathering from all over Number Four to see him. The thought made him grimace. These were only the first of too many ceremonies that he would have to wade through, like streams, on the way to where he wanted to go.

He had put off the meaningless honors, the public displays of adoration, for as long as possible, using his wound and his weakness as excuses. But he had spent the hard-won privacy of his convalescence working obsessively, trying to put what was left of his personal life in order before he became public property forever. He knew what he would see if he faced himself in a mirror; he had not gone near one since his release from the hospital. But he had endured far worse things than his own reflection too recently to let it bother him, or stop him. There had been no time for weakness, or pain, or doubt . . . there never would be again.

He moved back to his desk. His hand reached for the speaker plate at last; hesitated, as more seconds slipped by. The judgment he was about to pass was only a formality, a decision made weeks ago concerning an act that should have been done years ago. And yet . . . he needed more time.

He touched the speaker plate. "Ossidge. I'm still reviewing the evidence. I'll let you know when I'm ready."

"Right, Inspector." There was no discernible emotion in the disembodied voice, even though his sergeant had been waiting for more than an hour down in the detention wing. Ossidge was a phlegmatic lump, stolid and unquestioning. Gundhalinu tried to imagine what Ossidge would make of World's End, or what it would make of him. The irresistible force and the immovable object. But then, he couldn't imagine that Ossidge would ever even dream of making that trip; making the Big Mistake. . . .

He dropped into the seductive softness of his desk chair, letting it re-form around him. *Just for a moment.* . . . Just for a moment adrenaline stopped spilling into his bloodstream, and he was vulnerable. If he could only close his eyes, empty his mind and meditate, have one uninterrupted moment of peace, before . . . He pushed himself up out of his seat angrily, wincing as the abrupt motion hurt the half-healed wound on his side. He forced the pain out of his mind, as he had done over and over again for the past month.

He *needed* this time, this final stolen hour, for something more important than rest. So much had changed, and was about to change, in his life. He needed time to remember who he was.

He touched his belt buckle, pressing the hidden speaker button on its built-in recorder. The recorder had a direct memory feed, which he had used when he had kept the journal—to keep it private, pointless mental digressions and all. But now he left it on VOICE, hearing it mimic his own speech, the sounds familiar yet sufficiently distorted to seem almost impersonal.

The voice said, "Today I arrived at World's End. . . ."

He turned back to the window, frowning at the raintracks on the pane. *Rain again. Doesn't it ever stop?* But he knew the answer. *No more than time does.* He sat down on the deep sill, resting his forehead against the glass, letting the utter exhaustion of his body and mind hold him there. He watched as his breath condensed into fog, obliterating the present, and felt the empty room behind him fill up with ghosts.

DAY 1.

Today I arrived at World's End. It's still difficult for me even to believe I'm thinking those words.

But I've decided to record everything I experience here, as completely as possible. The notes of a reasonably objective observer can only be an improvement over the mass of lurid misinformation about this place. And if anything should happen—never mind. . . .

The shuttle trip from Foursgate was uneventful to the point of tedium. I could almost have believed that I was simply another tourist sightseeing on a strange world . . . except that there were only two other people on the flight, and neither one of them looked pleased about their destination. I didn't speak to them, and they returned the favor. The sky was overcast for almost the entire trip; I saw nothing of the world so far below. For all I knew we could have been circling Foursgate for two hours instead of covering half a planet.

When we landed the terminal was exactly like half a dozen others I've seen here on Number Four—a masterpiece of the banality that passes for modern on this world. The planetwide Port Authority runs its franchises with the same mindless efficiency wherever they are—even at the end of the world.

As I crossed the invisible climate-control barrier that separated the terminal from the real world outside, I finally began to realize that I had come to World's End . . . I had really made the Big Mistake.

The heat was suffocating. The air was so thick with moisture and strange odors that breathing itself was difficult. I dropped the bags that held the few belongings I'd brought with me, and looked for some sort of transportation. If there was anything, even a ground vehicle, it wasn't running. The two locals who had been on my flight passed me wordlessly and began walking away down a cinder track. I thought I could see some sort of buildings in the distance, which I assumed were the town. A jungle of unwholesome-looking plant life pressed in on the road and the terminal. There were black scorch marks where the flora had been burned back recently along the roadsides. I took off my heavy jacket, picked up my belongings, and began to walk.

I stopped again as I reached a gateway at the edge of town.

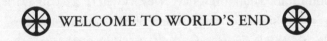

WELCOME TO WORLD'S END

Someone had scrawled on the blistered wall, complete with the official seals:

THE ASSHOLE OF THE HEGEMONY.

It struck me like a slap in the face, a grotesque insult. I stared at it until the tension of my clenched jaw made my face hurt—made me remember who I'm not, here. I said to myself, "It's not your problem."

I looked through the gateway, feeling as if someone were watching me. But the shuttered whiteness of the street was empty; the buildings lay dazed in the insufferable humidity of the early afternoon. I stood there awhile longer, feeling the sweat crawl down my chest beneath the coarse cloth of my loose blue tunic; suddenly I longed for the security of a uniform. My head began to throb with the silent rhythm of the heat . . . and all at once the whiteness of the street seemed to shimmer and re-form as endless fields of snow. A mirage, a hallucination—I've seen it a hundred times. You'd think a sane man would be able to put it out of his mind, after so long. . . . I hunched my shoulders, feeling a chill as I went on through the gate.

The first thing I did in the town was buy a sun helmet and a drink of cold water—they don't give away anything here, not even water. This is the Company's town, as the shopkeeper informed me, not a resort. The conglomerate that controls World's End is known as Universal Processing Consolidated, back in Foursgate. But out here they are simply the Company, the only, and they've grown bloated and corrupt on their monopolistic exploitation. Their presence is everywhere as you walk the streets—on signs, on people's lips, on their dreary uniform coveralls. No one looks at anyone else for longer than they have to here; but I still felt as though hidden eyes followed me constantly.

This town seems to have no name. It certainly has no individual identity. It exists to serve the Company, as a supply center and as a bottleneck for the countless fortune hunters drawn to World's End year after year—all of them certain they'll be the ones to strike it rich. The Company tolerates a limited number of independent prospectors who want to explore the wilderness, who are willing to run risks that even the Company won't in searching out resources. It takes no responsibility for their fates, but it takes half of their profits, if any. They get their permits here; I suppose I'll have to enquire about that.

World's End is an obsession for too many of them, the fools. I suppose it's worthy, even fitting, that it should be. World's End is a canker at the heart of Number Four's largest continent, millions of kilometers of terrain that are still virtually unknown after centuries of Hegemonic control. There's been good reason to explore it, and to believe in the tales of fortunes for the taking; the Company is proof enough of that. The profits they've taken out of the wastes have made Universal Processing more powerful on Number Four than anything but the Planetary Council. Rich ores lie hidden out there, veins of precious minerals, fist-sized gemstones—unimaginable wealth.

But while the wasteland flaunts its treasures, it defies human efforts to fully exploit them. Even the Company is powerless in the end, in World's End. At the center of the wasteland is Fire Lake, a vast sea of molten rock seeping up out of the planet's core like blood from a wound. Official reports would have one believe that it's no more than a weak spot in the planetary crust. But they don't—can't—explain the bizarre electromagnetic phenomena that spread out from Fire Lake: distortions that corrupt instrumental readings and turn their carefully collected data into gibberish. There are half a hundred unofficial explanations as well, which claim that Fire Lake hides everything from a black hole the size of an atom to the gateway to hell.

None of the explanations satisfies me any better than having no explanation at all does. Ever since I've been on Number Four I've thought that if they'd bring in the best equipment—and

Kharemoughi Technicians to operate it decently—they'd get the truth. The Company has poured fortunes into a solution and come away with nothing. Even the sibyls couldn't give them an answer—and sibyls are supposed to be able to answer any question. Probably they just haven't asked the right ones.

If a decent answer existed, there wouldn't be any mystery to confound the Company or lure an endless stream of self-deluded wretches into itself and swallow them whole. Hundreds of people disappear out here every year, and are never heard from again. . . .

If a decent answer existed, I wouldn't be here, waiting to follow them. I don't belong in this sweltering hole, with a lot of bloody fools and fanatics, all searching for an escape from responsibility or from the past; for a handout from fate, for answers without questions. I'm not like them. I have no choice about being there, duty and family honor demand it.

My brothers are the self-deluded fools. They've been missing out there for the better part of a year now. Difficult to believe, when it seems like only yesterday that I looked up and saw them standing before me, as unexpected as ghosts. I can still hear their voices, every word of the incredulity that passed between them as they saw the scars on my wrists. *"Gedda. Gedda . . ."* they whispered, repeating the hateful name that I so justly deserved.

I turned my back on them, staring out at the city through the windows of my office, waiting until their voices died of shame.

They wouldn't ask me the reason for the scars, why I still bore them, why I still lived. Nothing in the code of our class tells them how to ask. So I faced them again, finally, and asked them what they were doing here on Number Four, years away from the family estates and holdings back on Kharemough. "And what do you want from me?"

"Do we have to want something besides to see you, after so long?" HK asked inanely.

"Yes," I said.

And so SB said, "We've come to make our fortune. We were only passing through here, anyway. We're on our way to World's End." Anticipating my disapproval, he tried to stare me down, still the impulsive bully.

I've faced down a lot of stares like that in the years since I left home. "Don't try to feed me sand, SB," I told him. "Some of us do grow up."

His pale freckles reddened. "I'd forgotten what a self-righteous little bore you always were."

I hadn't forgotten anything. I kept the desk terminal like a barrier between us. "You know, they have a name for what you plan to do, around here. They call it the Big Mistake." I turned to HK, still surprised to see graying hair above that familiar, self-indulgent face. The florid, shining-surfaced robe he wore hardly flattered his obvious bulk. I wondered why he didn't wear the traditional uniform that was his proper dress as head of family. "I'd expect him to make a mistake that big. But I never thought I'd meet you halfway across the galaxy from our ancestors, or the . . . your estates." I cleared my throat. "Things must be better than I remember, if you can leave your business holdings headless for so long. Or do you have a spouse by now, and an heir?" The sublight trips to and from the Black Gates added up to several years passed at home before they could return. I try not to keep track of the relativistic time lags that separate me from my past—it becomes an exercise in masochism too easily—but I knew that nearly two decades had passed on Kharemough since I'd last prayed at our family shrine. Since the last time I saw my father alive. . . . Memory stabbed me with sudden treachery, showing me a face—a woman's face, her skin and hair as pale as moonlight, the trefoil tattoo of a sibyl on her throat. The face I always saw when I tried to see my father's face, ever since Tiamat. I looked up at my brothers, my own face hot.

But HK was staring at the backs of his hands as though they belonged to a stranger. "No heir . . . and no estates."

"What?" I whispered. But one look at their faces and I knew. I leaned on the desk, straining forward. *"No."*

". . . lost them . . . bad investments . . . didn't foresee . . . SB's associates . . ."

I could barely focus on HK's words. The diarrhea of his excuses told me nothing, and everything. Images of Kharemough filled my mind: my world, the only world, the only life worth living. The life I've given up forever, because of my scars. I'd been able to live with its loss only because I could believe that whatever shame I'd brought on myself, my family's reputation remained untouched, the memory of my ancestors immaculate, as long as I stayed away. Their continuity and their ashes lay securely in the land that had been my family's since Empire times—proof of our intellect and our honor. But now, after so many centuries, our estates belonged to someone else . . . and so did our heritage. Some social-climbing lowborns with money for honor burned incense to my ancestors; claimed my family, with all its accomplishments, for their own. A thousand years of tradition destroyed in a moment. And all because of me.

". . . barely had the funds to finance this trip . . . World's End . . . only hope of ever recovering the family holdings . . . help us regain the estate, and the honor . . ."

A silvery chiming broke across HK's words, silencing him. He reached into the pocket on his sleeve distractedly and pulled out the watch. The heirloom watch, the Old Empire relic that my mother had restored and given to my father for a wedding gift. It must have been an anachronistic curiosity even when it was new—a handheld timepiece, that did nothing but tell time. Even my mother hadn't been certain how old it really was. As a child I had played with it endlessly, obsessed by all that it stood for. I could still see every alien creature engraved on its golden surface, feel the subtle forms of limb and jeweled eye under the loving touch of my fingers. The watch was the one remembrance that my father had left specifically to me in his will. But HK had kept it for himself.

"Get out." I held my voice together somehow as I touched my terminal, opening the door behind them. "Get out of here, before I . . ." Words failed me. "Go to hell in your own way! I don't want to know about it."

HK drew himself up like a beached clabbah, straining for dignity. "I should have known better than to appeal to your honor." Failing at dignity, and at irony.

SB caught HK's arm and pulled him toward the open door, glancing back once, to spit at me, *"Gedda."* And after that I didn't hear from them again. I told myself good riddance.

But instead of forgetting about them, I've followed them into World's End. I can't believe I've done this . . . the thought of just spending a night in this squalid town is enough to make any reasonable person take the next shuttle back to civilization. And it's not as if they went off for a holiday week and forgot the time. They disappeared, into an uncharted wilderness! They were totally unprepared for what they did—neither one of them ever attempted anything more dangerous before this than spending all day in the baths. If the wasteland didn't kill them, the human animals who inhabit it probably did, and picked their bones for good measure. Am I really going out there to let the same thing happen to me—?

When I was a boy, my nurse told me stories of the Child Stealer, who stole highborn babies and replaced them with cretinous Unclassifieds. For years I was sure that it must have happened to HK and SB. . . . They chose their fate, and if World's End swallowed them without a trace, they got what they deserved. They left no one and nothing behind, except me . . . left me with nothing but memories.

But since they're gone I'm head of family now . . . a title as hollow as it is unexpected. And they are still my brothers. That makes it my duty to search for them; my responsibility to all our ancestors—who will be my ancestors forever, whatever strangers violate my family's honor and claim my blood as their own. But still, if it weren't for Father, for what I owe to him . . .

If it weren't for me, none of this would have happened.

But even if I'm a failure, I'm not a fool. I have training that HK and SB never had, I have the experience to help me search for them. This isn't impossible. . . .

Besides, if I left here now, what would I go back to? My job? I can't even do that competently anymore. They don't want to see my face back in Foursgate until I can perform my duties again. Ever since my brothers came to this world, I've felt as if I've lost all control of my life.

I've got to give myself enough time for this search—time to find out what it is I've lost, and how to get it back . . . to find out whether it even matters.

DAY 7.

Gods, can it be a week already since I came here? It seems like forever—and yet it seems like only yesterday that I made my first trip to the Office of Permits.

I was informed by the slovenly woman who rented me my vermin-infested room that I would need clearances. Even to stay here in town longer than overnight I would have to have a Company permit—and to enter World's End, I'd need to get half a dozen more. When I heard the news I was elated, because I realized that my brothers would have had to do the same thing, and that there would at least be some record of how and when they left here. I actually thought that this was going to be easy.

In the morning I went into the center of town. But the moment I crossed the threshold of the Permit Office on the town square, I realized that my preconceptions about anything being reasonable or easy here were fantasies. There was no door on the office; the heat was worse inside than outside, though I wouldn't have believed that was possible. There were no chairs, no counters, nothing but a clear wall dividing the single room in two.

Beyond the wall I saw three people standing or sitting in the real office, which looked primitive but functional. I crossed the room to the wall and rapped on it. Only one of the clerks even bothered to glance up at me; none of them came to the wall. I rapped on the wall again, harder, as I realized they were ignoring me. She waved a dismissing hand, as if she were involved in something important. She was not doing anything at all that I could see.

Another obvious outsider came into the office and stood at the wall beside me, holding up a credit disc. He shouted something that sounded like "Moron!" One of the clerks, an old man with a face like a slice of dried fruit, crossed the room to us at last. He struck something against the wall and I heard a single note chime; abruptly there was a window open in front of the other man. A breath of cool, dry air touched my face.

"Excuse me," I said, "but I was here first."

"Wait your turn," the clerk snapped at me. The other man grinned, holding his spot, as the clerk took his credit.

I waited, trying to control my anger at being treated like the lowest Unclassified back on Kharemough. The other man finished his business at last, and I leaped to take his place before the clerk could close the window again.

"I need . . . I need some information," I blurted. "I'm looking for my brothers—"

The clerk cocked his head insolently. "They're not in here, sonny. Go back where you come from, you'll find all the brothers you want." He wheezed with silent laughter.

I took a deep breath, and said, as evenly as I could, "My brothers . . . were here about a year ago. I believe they went into

World's End. They didn't come back. I'm here to search for them. I understand that I need some kind of permits to do that. I'd like to apply for them."

He turned away from the window without a word; but it stayed open and so I waited. He came back with a fistful of printout sheets. "Fill out these." He shoved them through at me and closed the window.

"You mean write on this? By *hand?*" I said. But I was already talking to his back. I looked around the empty office, searching futilely for a seat or a table. The room had not miraculously produced any, and so I leaned against the wall, filling out forms in quadruplicate for an hour with a broken stylus I found on the floor in a corner. By the time I was through detailing my business, requesting permissions, swearing solvency and sanity and revealing details of my physical and mental condition that were not even a physician's business, I had begun to think that the Company was a more formidable foe than any I'd ever meet in World's End. I wiped the sweat from my eyes for the hundredth time. There were still blank spaces left unfilled on half a dozen sheets, affidavits unattached, data unconfirmed. I went back to the wall. "Moron!" I shouted.

The clerk answered me almost promptly this time. He took my papers and frowned and shook his head. "These aren't completed."

"I know that," I said, barely civil. "It's impossible. I couldn't get everything you want there if I spent a month back in Foursgate. . . . I'd have to send to Kharemough! I can't wait years—"

He shrugged, picking at his hangnails; the forms rustled. I could smell him, a faint musty smell riding the cool air. "Should have come better prepared." He looked up at me as if he expected to see something that wasn't on my face. When he didn't find it, he shuffled the papers again. "Well . . . might be a way around some of these things here . . . might be some things we could do for you . . . might be some things we could overlook. . . ." He looked up at me once more, expectantly.

I didn't answer, not understanding what he wanted.

Finally he said, "It'll cost you."

I stiffened. "You mean a bribe? You expect me to pay you off, is that what you mean? I want to speak to your superior, Moron."

"Morang," he said coldly. "I'm in charge here. And I don't like your attitude. The Company doesn't have to do anything for you, you understand? Nobody needs you here; your kind is as cheap as dirt. We let you explore Company territory out of our generosity, and if you're not willing to give and take a little, you can just take the next shuttle out of here."

The irony struck me so hard I almost laughed. Fortunately I did not. "How much are your . . . fees?" I asked sourly.

"Ten for the first week's residency permit here in town."

"Ten?"

"Fifteen, for every week after." He looked at me. This time I kept my mouth shut.

"The clearances and permissions for you to actually enter World's End to prospect—or for whatever purposes you claim here—are more complicated. They take time, they've got to pass through a lot of hands. . . . Some of the security people might want to interview you in person—" He raised his eyebrows significantly; I bit my tongue. "Just to get you started, with all the data you're missing, is going to cost you fifty." He put out his hand.

My own hand tightened around my credit disc. "In that case, before I pay you anything, I at least want proof that my brothers actually went into World's End. I expect you can look that up in your datafiles."

"It's not permitted—"

"For a fee." I held my credit out in front of him.

"I suppose I can make an exception. Names?" I gave him their names and my credit, and he went away again. After another interminable wait he came back. He shoved a printout through at me, as if he knew I would only accept hard copy.

The data told me that my brothers had gotten their permits from the Company, and their clearances, and their supplies. How much it had cost them was not listed. They had gone into World's End about a month after I saw them. That was all. "Is this really all of it? Can't you tell me how they were traveling, or which direction they went, at least?"

He shook his head. "You got what you asked for." He handed me back my credit disc.

I glanced at my balance, and grimaced. "I guess I did." He frowned; my sarcasm was not lost on him, at least. "When can I expect to get my clearances?"

"Come back in a couple of days. Maybe something will be ready by then. There'll be more fees due." He took a long look at me. "But if I were you, I wouldn't count on leaving here soon." He shut the window with another crystalline note, and walked away.

And every time I go there Morang tells me, "Come back in a couple of days." There are always more fees, but nothing to show for them. And every time I go in he laughs up his sleeve at me again. I'm a marked man. I know I'm not playing this game right . . . but damn it, I wasn't born to sycophantry and bribery, the way everyone in this town seems to have been!

If only there were some other way into World's End—but the

Company monitors its perimeters with heavier surveillance than most lawful governments do. This is the only rational way.

My brothers came this way, and they escaped this bureaucratic maze, at least. There has to be a way for me to find their trail from here, and follow it. Patience, that's all I need. Perseverance. Logic.

Damn it! Bug spray.

DAY 14.

Today began like yesterday, and the day before. I made the ritual bureaucratic homages one more time, trying to get my clearances—getting nothing but heat stroke and a thirst. After that I started back to C'uarr's place in the Quarter; another ritual programmed into my feet by now. I swore I wouldn't go to C'uarr's today . . . swore I'd be sick to my stomach if I even saw another glass of his rotgut liquor. But I went there anyway.

The sudden darkness of the bar is as blinding as the street. I always stop inside the doorway, pushing back the sunshield of my helmet, blinking until my eyes can fill in the tableau of the barroom regulars. The handful of outsiders in their foreign clothes stand out among the Company workers like bits of colored glass in a bed of smooth white stones. Always the same strangers—trapped like me in this purgatory I've begun to think of as the Wait.

"Still here, pilgrim?" a hulking Company guard asked me as he crowded me aside from the entrance. He stopped, grinning down at the indignation I couldn't quite disguise. A lifetime won't be enough time to make me suffer gracefully the insults of inferiors. "How long's it been for you?" he asked. When I didn't answer, he said, "Well, maybe tomorrow. Or maybe not." He laughed, showing yellow teeth.

I stood out of reach of his meathook hands. A few days back I saw two guards casually break all the fingers of a prospector they claimed was cheating at five-and-twenty. The Company is its own law when you reach World's End, and the law changes on a whim or with a mood. The uniform law of the Hegemony is only a memory here.

The guard moved on, and I went to the bar. I ordered a drink too loudly, and had to endure C'uarr's smirking, slow-motion response. C'uarr, the one-eyed, is as bitter and corrosive as his poisonous liquor. He's not a local—from Samathe, probably, by the name. I used to wonder what kept him here, when he plainly hates this town and what he's doing, just like he hates everyone who comes into this place. As the days passed and stagnation began to eat at me I started to think he was a parasite who lived on the misery of the Wait more than on any money it brought him. Today it occurred to me that he stays simply out of inertia.

C'uarr slammed the squat glass down on the filthy bar; droplets of red liquor bloodied his hand. His hand reached out, palm up as always. I flipped him a marker. "Any word?" I asked as I took my drink. I'd paid him to ask around about my brothers. But the question was rhetorical by now; I turned away even before I heard the answer. It was always *no*. I felt C'uarr's stare follow me, full of mockery and dark speculation. He's like an animal—he senses that I'm not really the same as the others. I can tell when he looks at me.

The low-ceilinged room stinks of mildew and fesh sticks. No one else bothers to glance up as I make my way to a bench at an empty corner table. I've faded into the background, just like they have. *Pilgrims,* the Company workers call them, and laugh. They make their pilgrimage to this place from all over the planet, from all over the Hegemony—seekers after legendary wealth, hidden treasure—all believers in the same religion, greed. Most of them end up in this trap instead, caught like bugs in a bottle while C'uarr and the Company bleed them dry.

I spent the rest of the afternoon sitting, staring, nursing that one drink until C'uarr threatened to throw me out. I ordered another, but didn't let myself drink it. The cheap, ruby-red local liquor is fermented from some kind of fungus. It's called *ouvung.* A dead worm drifts in every bottle. The first time I took a sip of it I gagged—and wondered whether the worm wasn't really there as a testament to the stupidity of its drinkers. I got used to it, just as they all do.

Finally the sky beyond the doorway began to darken. I ate another cheap, repulsive meal, and went back to my bug-infested room to sleep for the night. I've spent more on bug spray and sonic screens since I got here than I have on food. But I have to get some sleep . . . so that I can get up and perform this futile round over again tomorrow, and the next day, and the next. . . .

Sometimes I think I must be crazy to stay here . . . whenever I consider the odds against finding my brothers' trail in all that nothingness, in all of World's End. No one I've questioned here even remembers seeing them. Why in the name of a hundred ancestors couldn't HK have married decently, and had half a dozen heirs? Maybe one of them would have been halfway intelligent. . . . SB talked him out of it, I'll warrant; the way he talked him out of every other sensible thought he ever had. Though what woman would have either one of them? Even our own mother. . . .

You idiot—if you ever do get clearance from the Company to enter World's End, what the hell will you do with it?

DAY 21.

Three weeks.

Three weeks in this outhouse, and more money wasted already than I earn in half a year. Gods, even Tiamat was better than this. So today I celebrated . . . with a whole bottle of C'uarr's rotgut to keep me company. He must've talked me into it. He cheated me, though. I paid for a full bottle, but he gave me this empty, without even a worm. . . .

Damn it, I know I only had a couple. . . . I'm not a drunkard. I never touch liquor. Drunkenness disgusts me. It's a sign of weak character. I hate drunks. I ought to. The gods know I have to deal with enough of them . . . used to. Not anymore.

Not since a month ago. . . . It should have happened years ago. The message from the Chief Inspector on my screen. When I saw it I wanted to run away, like a child, because I knew there was only one reason he'd ask me to report to him in person. But my body got up from behind my desk and took me to him; it made the correct salute, as if my face wasn't betraying it with a look more guilty than a felon's.

Chief Inspector Savanne is not an easy man to face, even on a viewscreen. He returned my salute, studying me with an uncertainty that was harder to endure than the cold disapproval I'd been expecting.

"Sir—" I began, and bit off the flood of excuses that filled my mouth. I looked down along the blue length of my uniform at my boots. I saw a hypocrite and a traitor wearing the clothes of an honest man. I'm sure the Chief Inspector saw the same thing. *Tiamat.* The word, the world, were suddenly all I could think of. *Tiamat, Tiamat, Tiamat. . . .*

"Inspector." He nodded, but all he said was, "I think we both realize that your work has not been up to standard in recent months." He came directly to the point, as usual.

I stood a little straighter, forcing myself to meet his gaze. "Yes, sir."

He let his fingertips run over the touchboard of his terminal, throwing random messages onto its screen, as he did sometimes when he was distracted. Or maybe the messages weren't random. "You obviously served very competently on Tiamat, to have risen to the rank of Inspector in so short a time. But that doesn't surprise me, since you were a Technician of the second rank. . . ." He was also a Kharemoughi, like most high officers in the force.

Were. I swallowed the word like a lump of dry bread. My hands moved behind my back; I touched my scarred wrists. I could protect my family from shame by staying away from home. But I had never been able to forget my failure; because my people would never forget it, and they were everywhere I went.

He glanced up, frowning slightly at my surreptitious movement. "Inspector, I know you carry some unpleasant memory from your duty on Tiamat. . . . I know you still bear the scars." He looked down again, as if even to mention it embarrassed him. "I don't want to know what happened to you there, or why you haven't had the scars removed. But I don't want you to think that I hold what you did against you—"

Or what I failed to do. The very fact that he mentioned it at all told me too much. I said nothing. I felt my face flush.

"You've served here on Number Four for nearly five standards, and for most of that time you've kept whatever is troubling you to yourself. Perhaps too much to yourself. . . ."

I knew some of the other officers felt that I was aloof and unsociable—and I knew that they were right. But it hadn't mattered, because nothing had seemed to matter much to me since Tiamat. I felt the cold of a long-ago winter seep back into my bones as I stood waiting. I tried to remember a face . . . tried not to remember it.

"You've shown admirable self-discipline, until recently. But after the Wendroe Brethren matter. . . . It was handled very badly, as I'm sure I don't have to tell you. The Governor-General complained to me personally about it."

And the Police had to demonstrate the Hegemony's goodwill. My eyelids quivered with the need to let me stop seeing. But I held his gaze. "I understand, sir. It was my responsibility. My accusations against the Brethren's chamberlain were inexcusable." *Even though they were true.* But truth was always the first casualty in our relationship with an onworld government. Kharemough held the Hegemony together with a fragile net of economic sanctions and self-interested manipulation, because without a hyperlight drive, anything more centralized was impossible. The seven other worlds of the Hegemony were technically autonomous—Kharemough cultivated their sufferance with hypocritically elaborate care. I knew all of that as well as anyone; I'd learned it on Tiamat. "I should have offered you my resignation immediately. I've had—family difficulties the past few months. My brothers lost . . . are lost in World's End." I felt the blood rise to my face again, and went on hastily, "I don't offer that as an excuse, only as an explanation." The Chief Inspector looked at me as though that explained nothing. I couldn't explain even to myself the dreams that had ruined my sleep ever since my brothers came: the ghosts of a thousand dispossessed ancestors; the face of my father changing into a girl's face as pale as snow; endless fields of snow. . . . I would wake up shivering, as if I were freezing cold. "I offer you my resignation now, sir." My voice did not break.

The Chief Inspector shook his head. "That isn't necessary. Not if you are willing to accept the alternative of a temporary reduction in rank, and an enforced leave of absence until the Governor-General has forgotten this incident. And until your . . . emotional state has regained some kind of equilibrium."

If only I could forget the past as easily as the Governor-General will forget about me! I only said, faintly, "Thank you, sir. You show me more consideration than I deserve."

"You've been a good officer. You deserve whatever time it takes to resolve your problems . . . however you can," he said, uncomfortably. "Rest, enjoy this vacation from your responsibilities. Get to feel at home on this world." He glanced at me, at the scars on my wrists. "Or perhaps . . . what you need is to look into your brothers' disappearance in World's End."

For a moment I felt a black rush of vertigo, as if I were

falling—I shook my head, saw a fleeting frown cross the Chief Inspector's face.

"Come back to the force, Gundhalinu," he murmured. "But only if you can come back without scars."

Without scars . . . without the past. What's the point of having the scars removed? It would only be one more act of hypocrisy. I'd still see them. And so would he. Life scars us with its random motion. Only death is perfect.

DAY 22.

Gods, I can't believe what I did to myself yesterday. How could I have done something that asinine? I was sick half the night. I've never been drunk like that. It's this place. It must be.

This morning I swore to myself that if nothing changed today I'd give up this insanity. I'll never know if I meant it this time or not . . . because something finally happened.

I was back in C'uarr's place, as usual. A local man came over to me where I sat, nursing my drink and my queasy stomach. Finally I realized that he was interested in me, and I looked up at him. He was tall and heavyset, closing in on middle age, with skin the color of leather and straight black hair. A Company man, I thought . . . an ex-Company man. His dingy coveralls had no insignia or identification, only white patches that showed they'd been there once. A tarnished religious medal dangled against his chest; bitter lines bracketed his mouth. "You Gedda?" he asked.

I found my jaw clenching with resentment. I've gotten too

used to this enforced solitude. I worked my tongue loose, and said, "Yes." I go by Gedda here. It suits me better than my own name, and it hides my identity from chance encounters. My real identity is a liability in a place like this . . . and besides that, meaningless.

The man sat down without waiting for an invitation. I frowned, but said nothing. He stared at me, assessing me in turn. There was something disturbing about his gaze. "I hear you're a Kharemoughi. A Tech?"

I nodded. "I was once."

The hooded eyes dropped to the scars on my wrists. "What happened?"

I turned my hands over, palms down on the damp tabletop. "I got tangled up in Blue." The standard phrase for trouble with the police. I saw his mouth quirk.

"What are you doing here?" he asked.

"Waiting."

"Tired of it?"

I felt my skin prickle. I had come to the end of believing that I would ever get permission to enter World's End, ever master the rituals of whim and bribery that have confounded me all the while I've been here. And now this stranger seemed to be offering me clearance on a ceremonial platter. "What do you want?"

He said, "I want to go prospecting. My vehicle is a Company junker. They don't think it can be repaired. I think all it needs is somebody who knows his ass from a socket. I hear you Techs can fix anything. If you can fix this, we'll go together."

That was all he wanted. I let myself laugh. "If I can't fix it, no one can." I offered my hand. The stranger shook it, after the local custom. I asked, "What do I call you?"

"Ang," he said.

I finished my drink, out of habit, and we left the Wait together.

DAY 23.

I could hardly believe my luck this morning, when Ang actually showed up at my room with every permit and clearance I needed to get into World's End. After so many weeks of maddening bureaucracy, it was like being set free from prison. I didn't bother to ask him how he'd done it—there's only one way. No matter; it seemed like a miracle.

I should have known my good fortune was too perfect to be true. This afternoon Ang took me to see the vehicle—a triphibian rover, in bad shape but not impossible, if he can get me the parts I'll need. That's not the trouble. The trouble is that there are three of us, not two. Today I met the third man.

He seemed about as surprised to see me as I was to see him, even though he'd apparently been expecting me. He was waiting in a junkyard when I arrived with Ang, kicking at the fungal creepers that grew up through the sea of scrap metal.

Ang snorted with laughter as he saw the man kicking and cursing, as if discomfiture with the repulsive flora of this place were somehow amusing. "It'll all be back tomorrow," he said, to no one.

"Who's that?" I asked. The other man was peering out from under the wide rim of his sun helmet. His skin and hair were the color of paste, as if he was never outdoors by choice. His blunt, tight-muscled body gleamed with sunblock lotion and sweat. I distrusted him on sight.

"Spadrin," Ang said, or rather called out. "This is our mechanic."

"You mean he's a partner?" I asked. I was more than a little irritated. Ang hadn't mentioned a third partner, either this morning or when he'd asked me to join him. He'd offered me an equal share of anything we found—but he never mentioned that it would be a three-way split.

Ang didn't bother to answer me, now that the answer was obvious. And Spadrin was staring back at me in a way that made me forget about Ang's shortcomings.

"This is Gedda," Ang told him.

Spadrin started visibly when he heard the name, but then his frown came back. "You got a Kharemoughi? You said we were going to get some Company hand—" He broke off. "Why?"

"He was the best I could do." Ang shrugged, but it wasn't an easy motion. I wondered whether his comment was a compliment. His hands were making fists inside the pockets of his coveralls.

Spadrin glared at Ang, disbelief plain on his face. Then he looked me up and down pointedly, as if I were an inanimate object.

I stared back at him, reconfirming my first impression. He was clearly out of place. His clothes were made of a shining,

silken fabric, and might have passed for stylish summerwear in
some climate-controlled metropolis; but they were absurdly impractical here. The tattoos running up his bare arms told me a
lot more, although I recognized only a few of the designs and
symbols. They all have their separate meanings: they illustrate
a man's life history in the Hegemony's underworld. Spadrin was
a career criminal.

"What are you doing out here?" he asked me.

"The same thing you are," I said.

He didn't believe it, any more than I did. He looked at Ang.
"I don't want him."

"I do." Ang turned away abruptly. "Gedda," he said to me,
pointing at the rusty metal hulk rising up beside us, "take a look
at it, tell me what you need."

I moved warily past Spadrin, and began to inspect the vehicle. I heard the two of them arguing behind me as if I couldn't
hear them; listened while trying to seem like I wasn't listening.
Spadrin used the worldspeech of Number Four with surpris-
ing fluency. Anyone can learn a language quickly with an
enhancer, but only someone with some intelligence will speak
it well. Spadrin is not stupid . . . and I won't forget it. At last he
turned and strode away, cursing, and I finished my inspection
in peace.

"Well?" Ang said, when I climbed down from the cab.

"It's not hopeless." I leaned against the rover's pitted side and
wiped rust from my hands. "The power unit is sound. You said
you can get me tools and parts?"

He nodded.

"It's not going to be cheap—"

"I have contacts in the Company. I can get anything you

want." The last was said with something closer to arrogance than to confidence.

"Good, then. How much do you understand about how a rover functions?"

"A hell of a lot more than most people," he snapped. "I've been piloting them since you were a snot-nosed brat." As if somehow I was supposed to have known that. "Just tell me what you want."

I bobbed my head. "Then I'll be precise." I gave him my initial lists, being as technically accurate as possible, and watching him for signs of comprehension. ". . . And finally, but most importantly, I'm going to need a new repeller grid, if you want this thing airborne."

That got a reaction. "A grid? The grid is out?"

I nodded. "It's completely deteriorated. Believe me, you don't want to risk flight on it."

"By the Aurant!" His frustration was scorching. A grid would make the difference between swift, comfortable travel by air, and an endless, arduous land journey. All the difference in the world. But he only grunted. "I'll see what I can do." He reached into a pocket of his coveralls, pulled out a fesh stick, and stuck the piece of narcotic-soaked root into his mouth.

"Ang—"

He looked up sharply, as if he knew what I was about to say.

"Why didn't you tell me about Spadrin?"

He looked down again, lighting the fesh, and shrugged.

"Listen, Ang. . . ." I took a deep breath, trying to hold on to my patience. "This is a two-man vehicle. Three of us is going to make spending a lot of time in it damned uncomfortable. I know why you need me on this trip; but why him?"

"Protection."

"Protection!" It was the last thing I'd expected to hear him say. I almost told him that I was police-trained, that I could offer him better and surer protection than Spadrin ever could— but I didn't want to start him asking about my motives instead of Spadrin's. "Gods, man," I shook my head, "don't you know what Spadrin is?" I was sure Ang had never even been to Foursgate, let alone offworld. But spending his life here in this borderland, he must have seen hundreds of Spadrins passing through: on the run from the law, or looking for easy victims.

"He's an offworlder." Ang said it as if *offworlder* and *scum* were the same word. "He came to World's End just like you. Said he was stranded in Foursgate, needs a stake to get back to his homeworld."

"He's more than that." I couldn't keep my own voice from rising. "Do you know what those tattoos of his mean? He's killed more people than you have fingers to count them. He's wanted for crimes on most of the worlds of the Hegemony. If he's stranded here, it's probably because he's in trouble with his own kind, and he needs a place to cool out as much as he needs a stake. . . . He's going into World's End hunting fresh meat, and you'll be the first—"

"How do you know so damn much about it?" Ang said sullenly.

I hesitated, realizing that I'd said too much already. But he went on, before I had to answer. "He's no worse than the robbers and 'jacks we'll meet out there—and he'll be on our side."

"On our side?" I echoed incredulously. "He's on nobody's side but his own. He's a criminal, Ang! You're not protecting yourself, you're putting a target on your back."

"I'm not stupid." His jaw clenched stubbornly. "I know what I'm doing. He won't make trouble."

"You're deluding yourself. We have a saying on the . . . there's a saying, that a man who lies down with thieves is lucky if he ever wakes up again."

"You don't have to go with us." He pointed a thumb back toward town. "You can stay here."

My mouth tightened. "I'll go," I said, thinking, *But I'll sleep with my eyes open.*

"You'll go." His own mouth curved upward. "Just like all the rest."

DAY 32.

For the past week I've been trying to resurrect Ang's dead rover piece by piece, with whatever parts he can beg, borrow, or steal. He is an ex-Company man, as I'd thought; he must be calling in a lot of favors. He's gone most of every day, hustling up more parts—or maybe just avoiding us, I don't know. I don't think he cares much for either Spadrin or me; probably wishes he didn't need us. It's mutual. But sooner or later everything I ask for shows up at the junkyard, where the rover lies like some immense dead beetle. Every time I trip over supplies inside the sleeping cabin, I try to imagine what it will be like to share this vehicle with two other people, even for a few days. Someone is going to sleep on the floor; it isn't going to be me.

Working on the rover is almost a pleasure, after sitting in C'uarr's place for so long. Though if someone had told me ten years ago that I'd ever enjoy lying on my back in the mud, with lube sifting into my eyes, sweating and blistered like some common laborer, I'd have committed suicide. I . . . All in the line of duty, as they say. There are worse things than manual labor, and I've borne some of them, all in the line of duty.

Not that today was unique for its hard work. More for its tedium, while I waited for the replacement grid I need to get the rover airborne. I spent the morning rereading the last of the information tapes I'd managed to unearth in the pathetic local datacenter. I've had to learn about this vehicle the hard way; they've barely heard of reading out here, let alone memory augmentation. I finally finished everything, and settled into adhani meditation in the rover's shadow. Then Spadrin arrived. He kicked me in the thigh, and said, "Wake up, you lazy shit."

I lunged to my feet, my reflexes almost betraying my training as my hand reached for the weapon I no longer carry.

Spadrin stepped back, and I froze as I saw metal. The knife blade disappeared into the sheath hidden in his sleeve. He grinned faintly, as if he'd proved something.

Seeing him always makes me think of venomous insects exposed beneath overturned stones. This time he was wearing the loose-woven tunic and pants Ang had forced him to buy for practicality. He had a half-empty bottle of ouvung in his fist, as usual. He prodded the tape-reader I'd been studying and said, slurring, "You goddamn Kharemoughis make me sick. You think the universe's got nothing better to do than wait around till you feel like fixing it."

I reordered my tangled instrument belt. My hands ached from the need to make fists. He was drunk—I could have had him disarmed and flat on his back in seconds, but I can't afford to betray my police training. It would only make him more suspicious of me—and make it even harder to get the cooperation I need from Ang. I only said, "I told Ang I'll finish the work when he gets me the repeller grid. I never claimed to be a miracle worker."

"Then you're the first Tech I ever met who didn't." He began to turn away.

"Spadrin," I said, and watched him turn back. "Don't ever touch me again."

He grinned, and spat the iesta pod he'd been chewing on at my boot.

I began to tremble as I watched him go. The emotion was so strong I could taste it, like vomit. I wanted to . . . Gods, what's wrong with me—letting a degenerate like that drag me down to his level?

Ang must be blind.

DAY 33.

Something happened today, and I don't know what to make of it . . . except that I want to make it *mean* something.

This morning I heard Spadrin's voice at the edge of the scrapyard. I looked out of the rover's cab, afraid that he was coming to harass me again. But he was talking with someone else—I saw two figures swim in the heated air. The other person was a woman. I watched him push her away suddenly, so hard that she fell. He disappeared into the yellow-green jungle.

I crossed the field of rusting metal and fleshy weeds to help the woman up. As I saw her face I realized I'd seen her before. Last night she came to the door of Ang's place in the Quarter, while we were going over supply lists. Ang had sent her away angrily, and without bothering to explain anything to us.

"I'm all right . . . thank you," she said, obviously shaken. She wasn't what I expected at all—a small, neat woman in the usual loose white Company coveralls. Her face was bare, and her dark, graying hair was cut short. She was not young, though she was probably younger than she looked. There was an atypical air of gentility and dignity about her. I knew what she wasn't, but I couldn't guess what she was. She met my stare with her own, and said, "You're very kind." The words were like a judgment, or a benediction. "My name is Hahn—Tiras ranKells Hahn," last name first, after the local custom. "May I speak with you?" She sounded as if she didn't expect me to say yes.

But I said, "Call me Gedda," and I offered her my arm. She seemed grateful for the support as I led her back to the rover's shade. She sipped cold water from my canteen, buying time until she was ready to tell me what she wanted. I listened to the sounds of the day—the thrumming of a million heat-besotted tarkas, the jungle's sentient whisper, the clanking and grinding of the Company's refinery hidden behind high gray walls to our left. I uprooted a fat creeper that had spiralled up the rover's side since yesterday— I've never known a place where flora grows with such preternatural speed. I threw it away and wiped my hands on my hopelessly stained pants. If I live to see the Millennium, I may never be clean of the feel of this place.

"It's frightening, isn't it?" she said.

"What?" I asked.

"How precariously we float on the surface of life."

I grunted, looking at the jungle. "A functional repeller grid would solve that problem. What did you want of Ang?"

"His help. Someone's help. . . ." She rubbed her face. "My daughter Song . . . is missing. My only child."

"Have you reported—"

"You don't understand!" She shook her head. "She's gone to Fire Lake."

I laughed. Then I said, "Forgive me," at the sight of her face. "You couldn't know. You just struck a nerve: I've come here to find my brothers. It's been almost a year since they went

World's End. I don't know what happened to them. I don't even know if they're dead or alive. But they're all the family I have left. I have to find them; if I have to go into hell itself and drag them back—" I broke off, filled with sudden anger.

"Yes," she murmured. "Yes. You understand." Her callused hands clutched at her sleeves. "The need for *proof.*"

I frowned at her peculiar choice of words. "What do you want to prove? Whether she's all right? Whether she's dead?"

She stared at me. She shook her head again. "That I love her."

I felt my face go empty. I crouched down, pointlessly adjusting a dial on one of my instruments. I only looked up again when I was sure of my expression. And, looking up at her, I wondered what had drawn or driven her daughter into World's End.

"She isn't dead. I've had messages from her. But she . . . she isn't all right. Her mind . . ." Hahn's hand moved in vague circles, and her mouth pinched. "She says that Fire Lake speaks to her, through her. I can't bear knowing that she's out there, helpless. . . ." Her eyes were full of pain—and the one other emotion I always recognized. Guilt. "I want her brought back to me, if she can be made to come."

I sighed. "Why haven't you gone after her yourself?"

She looked away. "I can't. I'm needed here. The Company needs me, they wouldn't let me go out there. And besides, no one wants to take me."

Afraid, I thought. "What about her father?"

"Her father is dead." She looked down, and for a moment her face was bleak with memory. "He was so much like her. Neither of them ever understood. . . . I'm a sibyl, Gedda. And so is she." Hahn unfastened the high collar of her coveralls, and showed me her trefoil tattoo.

The shock of recognition left me speechless for a moment. I haven't been near a sibyl since . . . since I left . . .

The memory of another face, a young, shining face above that same tattoo, transfixed me. Snow, stars, the teeming streets of a city at Festival time—another world filled my eyes. Tiamat. One stolen night, on a world I would never see again, came back to me in an excruciating moment of loss and longing. And as I remembered I felt the sweet, yearning body of Moon, who was as fair and as untouchable as her name, pressed against my own. She belonged to another man, I belonged to another world . . . and yet that night our need had fused our separate worlds and lives into one—

When I recovered my wits, Hahn was staring at me with open concern. I remember mumbling something, turning away to hide the sudden hot surge of desire the memory aroused in me.

Her hand reached out to me, drew back again, as if she were afraid that I feared her touch. Everyone knows there is no cure for the man-made Old Empire virus that turns a sibyl's brain into a biological computer port. And everyone knows the infection can drive an unsuitable host insane.

"It's all right . . . I'm not afraid," I whispered. Only her blood or saliva in an open wound could infect me. But I understood suddenly why Spadrin had reacted so violently—out of superstitious fear. And I saw Hahn through different eyes, now that I knew the Old Empire's eternal sibyl machinery had chosen her above all others for her humanity and strength of will. She was not like other human beings. If she was afraid to go after her daughter, it wasn't for the reasons I'd first imagined. "You know where your daughter is out there?" I asked finally, because I had to say something.

Hahn nodded, her face filling with relief as she saw that I was not rejecting her. "There's a—a place, a ruined city called Sanctuary, by Fire Lake. She's there."

"It really exists?" I'd read about the lost city, the way I'd read of Fire Lake itself—as a thing shimmering on the edge of reality, lost in a haze of legend. Supposedly it was a haven for criminals and degenerates fleeing from Hegemonic law, who preyed on fortune-seekers who struck it lucky.

Hahn nodded again. "I've seen it, through her eyes, in—in Transfer." There was a peculiar hesitation, as if she were leaving something unsaid. "All they say about World's End is true: to stay there too long is to lose yourself forever." She glanced down.

I'd heard that radiation, or perhaps just the strangeness, caused physical and mental deterioration in people who spent too long out there. "Gone to Fire Lake" means "gone crazy" on Number Four. I shook my head. "I don't know how I can help you. I've come to search for my brothers, and I don't even know how I'm going to do that. It will take all the time I have, and more, just to pick up their trail in that wasteland. I'm sorry, sibyl."

I was ashamed to look up at her, ashamed to refuse a sibyl anything, even though logically I had no reason for guilt. Sibyls are the speakers of the Old Empire's preserved wisdom, the selfless bearers of an artificial intelligence that moves them in strange ways. They say that it is "death to kill a sibyl, death to love a sibyl, death to be a sibyl. . . ."

The memory of another time still lay like a cobweb across my mind's eye: the memory of another face, gazing up at me with eyes the color of moss-agate. The trefoil sign like a star on her ivory skin. The strength and wisdom that changed everyone she touched—

When I first met her I saw only an ignorant barbarian girl. But she was the child of a queen, about to become a queen in her own right . . . a sibyl, already fated for a destiny far greater than my own. I was the one who had been unworthy.

I forced my mind back into the present and watched Hahn try to control her disappointment. After a moment she asked, "Do you have a picture of your brothers? Perhaps I might have seen them somewhere around the town."

I pulled out the holo I carry with me and gave it to her. "They look younger there. It's an old picture." Once it had been a picture of the three of us. I'd had my own image removed.

She studied it, and nodded. "Yes . . . yes. I did see them. I spoke to them about my daughter. They were—" She glanced away, embarrassed.

I felt my face flush, as I imagined what SB's response must have been. "I apologize to you for their behavior, sibyl. They've brought enough shame on my family already to make the shades of our ancestors weep blood." I looked down, holding my scarred wrists against my sides.

"There's something more about them." She held the holo up, turning it in the light. "Yes . . . I've seen them since, somewhere else." She closed her eyes, frowning in concentration. "In Transfer . . . in Sanctuary."

Through her daughter's eyes, in the sibyl Transfer. That was what she meant. *A lead*, I thought, *a real lead, at last!* I exhaled, realized then that I had been holding my breath. A part of my mind resisted, telling me that this was too easy, that she could be lying out of self-interest—that even sibyls were human beings, not machines. I'd seen plenty of faces as open as hers hide every kind of lie.

But it was the only clue I had, genuine or not. It was

something, a place to start—the focus I so desperately needed for my search. Gratitude and hope shouted down my doubts; I felt my mouth relax into a smile for the first time in days. "Thank you," I said. "I'll go to Fire Lake, I'll find the city. I'll look for your daughter, and I'll bring her back to you if I can. . . ." I glanced away self-consciously. "Another sibyl—helped me, once. Maybe it's time I repaid my debt."

"Does Ang know that you're searching for something besides treasure?" Hahn asked.

I shook my head. "Not yet. He's a difficult man to talk to." It had seemed too awkward to try to explain the truth. I'd decided to wait for a better time.

"How will you get them to search for what you want to find?"

I laughed. "I'll worry about that after I get this damned thing running." I glanced at the rover, and back at her. "What about Ang, by the way?"

"What do you mean?"

"You came to his place last night. You know him?"

"We only worked together." She suddenly looked defensive. "I gave him assignments for years. I thought . . . he promised that he'd help me, when he was free of the Company. He said it so many times. But it isn't the Company he's belonged to all these years, it's World's End. World's End has poisoned him, just like—" Her mouth quivered. "Don't depend on him. And don't let it happen to you. Whatever you do, don't lose yourself in World's End."

I smiled again. "I have no intention of it."

She looked at me strangely for a moment, before she reached into the soft beaded pouch that she wore at her belt. She brought out two objects and gave them to me. One was a holo of a woman's face—her daughter, Song. The other was the trefoil

pendant of a sibyl, the ancient barbed-fishhook symbol of biological contamination that matched the tattoo at her throat. I'd
never held a sibyl's pendant, and for some reason I was almost
afraid to touch it now. I thought suddenly of the day, half a lifetime ago, when my father had sent me to one of the Old
Empire's choosing places. Just to stand before the place where
some ancient automaton judged the suitability of the future's
youth to become sibyls had paralyzed me. I had returned home
without ever entering it, and told my father that I'd failed the
test. . . .

Hahn stood waiting, still holding out the trefoil. I took it
gingerly, let it dangle from its chain between my fingers. A sense
of impropriety, almost of violation, filled me as I handled it. I
had no right to possess such a thing. "You want me to have this?
Why?"

"A talisman." She smiled, a little uncertainly. "And a proof.
Show it to my daughter, when you find her. Then she'll know
that you come from me." She gripped my hands suddenly.
"Thank you," she whispered. "For whatever you do, thank you
so much." Tears filled her eyes. "I love my daughter, Gedda, even
if she can't believe it. I feel her suffering, every day, and I'm helpless to stop it. Why did I ever . . ." She shut her eyes; tears ran
down her cheeks.

"Why did she leave?" I asked, realizing suddenly that there
was still more she hadn't told me.

But she only shook her head, turning away. "I don't know,"
she murmured. "Please help her—" Her voice broke into sobs.
She went quickly away from me, weeping uncontrollably, as if
her relief at finding someone to take up her burden had left her
defenseless against her grief.

I watched her until she was gone from sight, feeling a hard

knot of unexpected emotion caught in my throat. I looked down at the picture and the trefoil still lying in my hands, knowing that she hadn't given those things lightly to a stranger. She had told me the truth. She had lost her child, and her suffering was real enough. I know about loss. . . .

The trefoil threw spines of reflected light into my eyes, making them tear. I remembered suddenly how tears had come into my eyes on the day that I told my father I was leaving home . . . though I never imagined then that it would be forever. I would have broken down like Hahn, if I'd known—

It was hard enough to keep my composure as I saw his face. "How much . . . how much time have thou to spend with us, before thou must leave?" he asked me. He was standing in the High Hall, erect and dignified in the uniform that he wore even at home, the symbol of his pride as head of a family as old and honorable as any on Kharemough. But his voice sounded strangely weak as he asked the question.

"A little over a month." I smiled as I answered, trying to believe that it was a long time. The limpid counterpoint of a choral work by Tithane filled the silence between us, and eased the ache in my throat. I stared out the wide windows at the sky. Pollution aurora marred the perfect blue, a constant reminder of Kharemough's overworked orbital industries—the price we paid for our leadership in the Hegemony.

"We must notify thy mother. She will surely want to see thee once more . . . if her work will allow it."

I didn't answer, afraid that anything I said would be the wrong thing. Suddenly my chest hurt. I recited an adhani under my breath. Mother had gotten fed up with us all when I was only five. I could count on the fingers of my hands the times I'd seen her since then. She spent her time on another continent halfway around the world, leading archeological excavations of Old Empire ruins. . . . I had heard so many times as a child that I wasn't to blame that I was sure it must somehow have been my fault. She didn't come home before I left Kharemough.

"Are thou certain this is the right course? After all, thou're only a boy—" I saw the trembling of his hands, which he usually controlled so well.

"Father, I'm nearly twenty standards. I already have more degrees than HK and SB put together. I can't spend the rest of my life studying, preparing for something—" *For something I would never have.* "I'm a grown man. And I'm not thy heir. It would be dishonorable for me to live here any longer." But more than that, living with my brothers had finally become unbearable.

"Scholarship is a respected calling in its own right. Thou could at least remain here on Kharemough, and teach—"

"No." I bit my lip, seeing the pain in his eyes. But the pain of staying would be far worse.

"Thou know . . ." His mouth resisted the words. ". . . thou know that I'm not young. It's true that thou're last in line to inherit. But to leave Kharemough . . . If something were to happen to thy brothers—"

"Nothing will happen to them, Father." *If only it would!* The violence of the thought almost blinded me. I blinked and glanced away, afraid that he would read it in my eyes, and know. . . . "What could happen to them here?" With malicious spite, my mind showed me half a dozen fatal possibilities.

He shook his head, leaning against the ancient mantelpiece below the picturescreen. "What, indeed. A weakling and a parasite, left in control of our holdings when I'm gone." His hand clenched. "Thy mother has no interest in her responsibilities here. And without thee to oversee—"

"They won't listen to me when . . . when HK is head of family. It's better if I leave, better for the family."

He sighed. "If only SB had gone in thy place; as he should have, years ago. If only he had been born with thy sense of honor, or HK with thy intelligence. . . ." He looked up at me. "Or if thou had been born first." His eyes held mine, searching.

I took a deep breath, suddenly finding the courage to say what I had never dared to say before. "Father, I know the wisdom of the laws. They were intended to keep society in the control of the ones most capable of running it well. But . . . but here in our family, they don't . . . they don't seem . . ." I went on in a rush, "By our sainted ancestors, Father, can't thou disinherit them? It would be justice—"

"Enough!" He pushed away from the mantel, rigid with anger. "You've said enough! It's not in my hands. You will not mention it again."

You. Not *thou.* It stung like a slap. "Forgive me, Father." I bowed, whispering, "I had no right." I kept my burning face averted. "May I have . . . your permission to leave you?"

"No."

I started as I felt his hands on my shoulders. I looked up into his dark eyes as clear as garnets. He had been an old man when I was born, but now for the first time in my life I *saw* that he was old.

"Thou are all I have that makes me proud," he said, and he hugged me, for the first time since my childhood. I was so surprised that I almost pulled away. "I would give up my life for thee, gladly . . . but I cannot go against the laws." And yet his eyes implored me to understand something more—something that was beyond his power, but not beyond mine.

"I know," I said, answering only his words. I looked down. I still felt his touch, even after his hands dropped away. I gazed out the window at the gnarled gray stone of the pinnacle on which the main house sat. I felt the overwhelming weight of a thousand years of tradition pressing down on me, immobilizing me. "I—I would like to go down to the places of our ancestors now, and meditate."

He nodded, his face stern with disappointment. He turned away from me, leaning heavily against the mantel. "Yes. Say a prayer for us all."

I started for the door. He called suddenly, "Where will thou be stationed?"

"Tiamat."

"Tiamat!" He was himself again as I looked back at him. "The people there are little more than barbarians. I can arrange a better assignment for thee, one where at least thou will be dealing with civilized citizens—"

I shook my head. "No, Father. I chose this myself." Because it had seemed the most exotic, the most alien, among the choices I had: a world like something out of the Old Empire romances I read constantly.

Tiamat was a world of water and ice, whose small population lived mostly in a state of bucolic backwardness. There was only one major city on the entire world, a notorious tourist stopover—a fantastic relic of the Old Empire, called Carbuncle "because it was both a jewel and a fester." The Hegemony controlled Tiamat directly for a hundred and fifty years at a time, leaving the natives to fend for themselves for another century as Tiamat's twin suns entered the periapsis of their orbit around the black hole that was its stargate. Then gravitational instabilities closed the Gate to starship travel for a hundred years, and anyone left behind faced a lifetime of exile. Half the population of the planet became exiles, too, as they moved to higher latitudes to escape their suns' increased radiation. And the ritual of the Change sacrificed the Snow Queen, who had ruled for a hundred and fifty years, to the sea the Tiamatans worshipped.

The Hegemony wanted Tiamat, and wanted it completely under their control, for only one reason: the water of life. The longevity drug was distilled from the blood of mers, bioengineered creatures of the Old Empire that survived only in Tiamat's seas. The drug was extremely rare, so expensive that even for someone like my father it was only a dream. It made Tiamat worth keeping, and it gave me a chance to see a living city of the Empire. "It's my only chance to see the world where they find the water of life, before its Gate closes. And when it does close, I'll be reassigned. . . . It's not as if I'll be there for the rest of my life. I'll return home on leave—"

He smiled, to silence me. "I know thou will serve honorably, wherever thou go." The chiming of his antique watch made him glance down. His smile became an expression I couldn't put a name to. He took the watch from the pocket in his sash, where he always kept it. And that was the last time I saw it, until the day I saw it in my brother's hand. . . .

The junkyard and the clamor and the heat reclaimed me again—I almost welcomed them. I put the trefoil into my belt pouch, along with my brothers' picture. I glanced at the holo of Song. I saw a girl-woman wearing the familiar sibyl sign, with dark eyes and a mass of black hair. Somehow I hadn't expected it to be black. I stared at the image for a long moment, trying to find something in her face to tell me why she'd done what she had. Her eyes were disturbingly alive, as if even her image could see into other worlds. As if another woman, another sibyl, with hair the color of moonlight, could look out through her eyes in search of me. I jammed the holo into my pouch.

I don't know what to make of this. Things seem to fall into my hands even as they're slipping through my fingers. Just when it all seems hopeless, I'm given what I need—just as I was on Tiamat. And just when I think I'm safe, I remember Tiamat.

I remember that night, as if it were last night. I haven't thought of it in years. I wanted so much to forget that I really believed I had. I haven't even wanted a woman, since. . . . But tonight, gods—I ache for the feel of her body against mine.

Damn it all! Maybe I am crazy.

DAY 37.

We've begun our journey at last, for better or worse. We've been traveling upriver into World's End for nearly four days now.

Ang wasn't able to beg, borrow, or steal the grid I needed to get the rover's antigrav unit working, despite his assurances. That would have made everything a damn sight easier . . . but why should anything be easy when it all depends on the Company? In the end, Ang just seemed to run out of patience—as if he *had* to begin, as if he had to get back into the wilderness, no matter how he had to travel.

We've made the first part of the journey by water, our only other alternative. At least I was able to make sure this derelict is watertight. Thank the gods it held together—I was in no mood for bailing, let alone taking a swim in that foul yellow fluid. The stench was nauseating: the air purifier still needs overhauling. Spadrin actually got sick to his stomach from the smell and the motion of the water. Nothing seemed to bother Ang—not even the jungle pressing down to the shore on either bank, spilling into the river with a kind of frenzy, as if it were trying to reach us. It floats on the water surface, rotting and stinking and gray, like the flesh of corpses. Last night I dreamed about wanting to die, and not being able to . . . an old, old dream. I woke up and couldn't get back to sleep.

When I sleep tonight I suppose I'll dream about pumps. We reached the refinery today—the last outpost of the Company, and the last sign of "civilization" we'll see. Armed guards greeted us at the dock when we arrived. Fortunately Ang knew the password, or whatever it took for them to let us ashore. I never thought I'd be happy to be on Company ground again; but after four days on the river . . .

The sound of pumps is everywhere throughout the complex; there's no escape from it. This station sits—floats—in a vast, tarry swamp of petroleum ooze. Not even the jungle wants this stretch of ground. But the Company does. According to Ang they couldn't resist such a cheap source of hydrocarbons, so they built a pumping station and an entire bloody refinery on top of it. They thought it would be easier than fighting the jungle; now they fight day and night to keep the whole thing from sinking into the sludge. Why they didn't float the installation on repellers, I can't imagine. Any Kharemoughi could have told at a glance that it was absurd. I said as much to Ang as he showed me around.

He said, "Any fool could see it! But the Controllers wouldn't come and look for themselves. Now they've put so much in it they won't let it go. And they'll never build a new plant till they give up on this one. They don't really want to know what it's like here. They don't give a damn." He waved his hand, grimacing. Then he looked back at me and said, "You Techs like to point out the obvious, don't you?" As if I'd insulted him, even though he agreed with me.

I didn't answer. He frowned; then he shrugged and walked away. All day he'd shown a peculiarly territorial attitude about this place—especially considering that he seemed even more sour than usual upon our arrival here this morning. I watched him start up a conversation with a group of workers who were taking a break in the lifeless yard outside the refinery. Ang had been a geologist when he worked for the Company, and he knew a lot of the workers here. He'd arranged for us to stop over for a day, so that he could try one last time to locate a grid for the rover.

I wandered off alone across the yard, looking at the mega-lithic sprawl of the refinery. It occurred to me that I hadn't seen Spadrin all day; it was like being free of a physical weight. He'd stayed in our quarters, sleeping or drunk or just disinterested—there was nothing worth seeing by most people's standards. Primitive structures and monstrous entanglements of equipment all rusting, rotting, shored up or jury-rigged to keep them functioning. I was drawn to explore them by a kind of horrified fascination—and because I couldn't face going back to the claustrophobic hallways and the stupefyingly ugly rooms of the compound's living quarters.

But there was no real escape from the ugliness here. At last I heard Ang shouting at me, and made my way back across the yard. I climbed ladders and catwalks to the place where he stood with three of the workers, the highest point I'd reached yet in my exploration. I gazed at the geometric sprawl of the station silhouetted against the bleary red face of the setting sun; all I could see were towers thrusting black against the gray of the rising fog. Pale flames hovered at their tips as gases were wantonly burned off, adding to the stench that hung over this place day and night.

Ang said to the others, "This is our mechanic. Tell them what kind of grid you want."

I looked at the three Company men. One of them was a burly man wearing the orange coveralls of a supervisor. The others wore plain white—or what must have been white once. It struck me how hopelessly impractical it was to make them wear white in a place like this. To keep the cheap, untreated fabric from staining was impossible . . . and every new stain only reinforced the futility of trying.

The three of them looked at me with dark, disinterested eyes. It was hard to tell their faces apart, and Ang hadn't bothered to mention names. I gave them the specs on the grid I wanted, and the man in orange shrugged. "Maybe," he said grudgingly, as though he disliked the whole idea. A grid was not a small or inexpensive piece of equipment. "He can come with me and take a look, I suppose." He glanced at the others. "Randet? Filalong?"

One shrugged, the other shook his head. The one who'd shrugged came with us. Ang and the other man stayed where they were, lighting fesh. Smoking is strictly forbidden here. I was glad to get away from them.

I followed the other men along the catwalks, looking out at the blackwater swamp that lay beyond the refinery. The rotting sentinels of the jungle's edge waded like skeletons in the stagnant lake. "I'm Gedda," I said. The supervisor glanced at me. When it elicited no further response, I asked, "You have names?"

The supervisor frowned. "Ngeran. This is Randet. Ang said you're a Kharemoughi." It was merely a classification.

I nodded, and we walked on in silence. The others never bothered to look out, or down; they moved like sleepwalkers. I watched the sun disappear into the fog. Ngeran led us back down into the maze of buildings, stopping again and again to check on some project. After a while I began to suspect that he was stalling, probably hoping he could force me to lose patience and give up on the grid. But knowing the difference that grid would make in my life gave me the patience of the dead.

Everywhere he stopped, the workers would gather around and stare at me, sullen and uncertain. I made myself talk to them—trying to establish some sort of communication, to turn their hostility into at least marginal cooperation. It was like talking to a herd of animals. The only thing I could imagine these people relating to was their work, so I tried a few obvious questions about function, or process, or adjustment. They answered in monosyllables.

"You know," I said, studying a readout, "if you opened that line three-quarters, and decreased your input by about ten percent, this would actually produce more efficiently."

Something like interest began to show on a few faces. "That's slower," a man said, shaking his head.

"This class of machinery was designed to handle a maximum rate flow of about twenty-five. You only cause a backlog if you push it harder than that. Try it—you'll find you only have to recalibrate one time in ten."

"Really?" He stared at me. "How do you know that?"

"He's a Tech," Ngeran said, looking at me as if he saw me for the first time. I smiled.

Someone else touched my arm tentatively, to ask me about a different piece of equipment. I helped one worker and then another, answering their questions, offering suggestions when I could to make their work easier and more efficient. Most of them seemed grateful, unlike Ang. Now Ngeran was waiting for me, but his patience matched my own when he had something to gain from it.

By the time we reached the storage area, he seemed to have forgotten any resentment he'd felt at showing me what he had. I read eagerly through the supply listings he called up on the warehouse terminal, but there was no grid in the size range that we needed. I queried over and over, willing my eyes to see the listing I wanted.

"You don't have one," I said finally, hating to hear the words. My body suddenly felt heavy with fatigue.

Ngeran peered past me at the screen, double-checked the listing again. "We had one a few weeks ago. Or maybe it was a few months. . . . Guess it's gone." He straightened up and shrugged. "Sorry." He sounded sincere. "I don't care if I disappoint that dreamrider Ang. But I figure you earned a grid."

I grunted. Our last hope of getting airborne was gone. I thanked him for his trouble, and started to leave.

"Hey, Gedda—" he called after me. "You be around tomorrow?" There was an urgency in his voice that belied the casualness of the question.

I shook my head. Resignation settled into the heavy folds of his face. I left the building.

I wandered through the warren of passageways that led from one part of the complex to another, searching for the room we'd been assigned to. The sound of the pumps was everywhere, like the heartbeat of some giant beast. *How precariously we float on the surface of life*, Hahn, the sibyl, said. She might have been speaking of this place.

I tried to push her words out of my mind, but my disappointment over the grid brought them back again and again. I thought of our trip upriver, and what it said about the journey ahead. I wished profoundly that I had never left Foursgate, a place that was at least reasonably safe and comfortable. But there was nothing left there for me to go back to now.

I tried not to think about that, either—but in my mind I saw the river of circumstance that had carried us all inevitably to this place. I remembered Spadrin making an obscene pun of Foursgate, tying its name to the Gates—those black holes in space that give access to other worlds by swallowing our ships whole and excreting them halfway across the galaxy. To him Foursgate is a trap, not a haven. To Ang, World's End is a haven and a trap, sucking him into itself. . . . The real trap is the past; every choice we ever make leaves us fewer options for the future.

I thought of the grid again, and before that my decision to go with Ang, and before that my brothers. . . . I thought about leaving Tiamat, knowing I could never return. Leaving behind Moon—

Desperately I thought of the Hegemony's past, of my ancestors, those long-dead geniuses of the Old Empire who left us the sibyl network that had guided Moon toward some unknown destination. Who had solved the paradox of direct travel between the stars at faster than light speeds—who had been on the verge of discovering the key to immortality. Their Empire had collapsed of its own complexity, of too many wrong choices, before they could achieve that perfection.

And now their descendants and heirs yearn for those Good Old Empire Days—even as we try to rebuild on their ruins, with the help of the sibyls they left to guide us. "Come the Millennium!" we say—come the day when we have a real stardrive again, and the freedom to choose any world in the galaxy as our destination. Any world . . . even Tiamat.

I'll never live to see that day, and maybe no one else ever will. We're all victims of the past, and of chance. The nearest source of viable stardrive is in a system more than a thousand light-years away from Kharemough—and there is no Gate anywhere near it. The gods only know if the ships sent out nearly a thousand years ago will ever reach it, let alone be allowed to return with what we need. Such a great need, such a simple solution . . . and as impossible to attain as a grid to fit the rover.

By the time my mind had found its way back to its original problem, I realized that somewhere I had taken a wrong turn. My path led me down and down into the depths of the installation, into an underground populated only by machinery—engines, drills, and pumps, kilometers of conduit and pipe—all with a life of their own, self-guiding and self-servicing. I might have been the first person to set foot here in months, maybe years. . . . Or so I thought.

I was on a catwalk above an immense space where the sound of pumps was deafening, where the stench of asphalt and methane was suddenly, appallingly, fresh. Down below me lay a vast pool of steaming black ooze. Pumps disgorged excremental gouts of mud into the tank from half a dozen pipes. And then I saw something else, so small from where I stood that at first I couldn't be sure I really saw it: a line of human beings, moving like mindless insects, carrying buckets. They went to the tank and they filled up the buckets, and then they carried them away into the underworld, to some unimaginable destination. I stared down at them for what seemed like an eternity, and all the while the procession continued endlessly, and the level of the mud never changed. Beneath the white noise of the machinery, the figures moved like a silent procession of ghosts. The futility, the insanity, of what they were doing held me in thrall. I began to search for a way to get closer, to find an answer—a *reason*—for what I saw.

I turned where I stood—and found myself face-to-face with a uniformed guard.

"What are you doing here?" He caught me by the sweat-soaked front of my shirt.

I almost demanded to know what *he* was doing there, what those miserable wretches down below were doing—I caught myself just in time, remembering where I was, and how alone. I muttered, "I—I lost my way. I'm with Ang."

"Is that supposed to mean something? Get your ass lost again before I find you a bucket." He nodded at the railing, toward the mud. He shoved me.

I got lost again as quickly as I could.

It was well into the night by the time I found my way back to our assigned quarters. Ang had already returned, probably hours before; he lay sleeping in one of the bunks along the wall. Spadrin was sleeping up above him. I slammed the grilled door loudly enough to wake them up.

"Shut up, asshole," Spadrin grumbled, raising his head and letting it fall back.

Ang glared at me and sat up in his bunk, leaning out from under the edge of Spadrin's. "Where the hell have you been?"

"Paying a visit to the Underworld," I said irritably. "I think I know now where you people get your ideas about damnation—being forced to repeat the same futile, pointless task forever."

"What are you talking about?"

"Somewhere down in the bowels of this installation, I saw men hauling mud in buckets from a pool. In *buckets*. What the hell is going on here? What possible reason could there be—"

"Convicts," he said. "They're convicts. The government sends them out here, and the Company has to put them to work."

"Hauling mud? That's absurd. That isn't work, it's—"

"Punishment." He shrugged.

"But, ye gods, man, it doesn't help anybody! It can't possibly be efficient—a pipe would do the work ten times as well. And you could train those men to do something useful."

He stood up, towering over me. "There are more honest people than jobs out here as it is. You want more of them put out of work so a thief or a murderer can learn a trade?" The question was rhetorical. "By the Aurant, you sound like my wife! Nothing ever suited her, either."

I stared at him, amazed to think that he was actually married. He'd never mentioned a wife. . . . I'd never even wondered about his past. With some people it's easy to forget how much of another person's life lies hidden from view.

Ang laughed once, glaring at me with his head bent to one side. "What is it with you, Gedda? What are you really after out here?" This time he actually wanted to know.

I didn't answer, afraid to tell the truth, afraid he would leave me behind if I told him now that I wanted to go to Fire Lake.

"Yeah, Gedda," Spadrin goaded, "what are you running away from . . . what's your crime?" He pushed himself up again, watching me with hard eyes.

I looked down. "Impersonating a police officer." I turned away toward the lockers.

"Well, that suits." Ang's voice was sour.

I turned back. "What do you mean by that?"

"It suits your Technocrat arrogance. You Techs can strut around Kharemough like tin gods, but your gods or ancestors or whatever the hell you worship don't own this world. You make some damn good machinery, and you know how to tend it. But I heard you won't even talk to half the people on your own planet because they don't meet some half-assed standard of genetic purity. And you come in here and tell me the Company's not humane enough to criminals!"

It was the longest speech I'd heard from Ang since I'd met him. I couldn't begin to justify the complexities of Kharemoughi social structure to someone like him; I didn't even try. I merely said, "My being wrong doesn't make you right." His mouth snapped shut. I went on, as reasonably as I could, "If you find the Company so eminently fair, why aren't you still working for them?"

The frown settled more deeply into his face. He sat down again, tugging at his religious medal. He said, "I got sick of never getting rich . . . of finding more ways for some faceless bloodsuckers to get rich instead." He stared at the walls of the room, spoke to them, as if his voice could somehow reach through them into the depths of the installation. "My wife used to work here. She left, years ago, because she couldn't stand the Company anymore. She took my son. Said I was wasting my life. She was just like the Company: never satisfied. She didn't understand why I wouldn't leave. She didn't understand about World's End." He shook his head, as if he were shaking it free of ghosts. "No one understood why I go out there. Because you have to go *out* there to know her better than any human being. . . ." For a moment I thought he was still talking about his wife. "For years I saw the independents, those skywheelers and losers, trying to do my job . . . and some of them doing it! Getting rich off of World's End, instead of me. But I always knew she'd show me her heart someday. And then I—" He broke off, glancing around him. "We'll all be rich. I promise you that much." He actually smiled. It only made his face more expressionless.

"You have a real plan?" Spadrin asked. "What is it?"

I touched the pouch where I kept my brothers' picture, feeling tension tighten in my chest. If Ang had a definite plan in mind, that would make it much harder to get him to cooperate with my search.

But Ang pointed at the walls, shaking his head. He said in a whisper, "Not yet."

Spadrin frowned, but he nodded. I sighed, waiting to show Ang the picture, and tell him the truth as well. This was not the time. I wondered when the right time would ever come.

"What about the grid?" Ang asked me.

I shook my head. "They haven't got what we need."

"You're sure? You're really sure?"

I nodded wearily.

He muttered a curse, but his expression didn't change, as if it didn't really make any difference to him. "We'll leave at dawn, then." He looked back at me. "One piece of advice, Gedda. Don't try to find reasons for the things you see in World's End. Because there aren't any."

DAY 39.

We're crossing a range of mountains now. The jungles are finally well below us, thank the gods, but nothing has gotten better except the smell. At least Ang knows the passes; if he didn't, I wouldn't be able to tell the trail from the wilderness. If we'd only gotten that damned grid. . . . Oh, the hell with it. We crawl; I might as well get used to it.

We left most of the rain behind, along with the jungle. Ang says it just gets drier from here on. He ordered us to conserve water, even with the recycler. Unfortunately he seems to consider cleanliness in close quarters a luxury. I'm damned if I'll grow a beard.

Spadrin seems to have rights that Ang doesn't even give to himself. What the hell right does anyone have to take up storage space with crates of liquor and a full-spectrum video receiver when we barely have room to move inside the rover as it is? On top of that, he's a plughead. He spends half his time buried in that obscene device, overtaxing the rover's power systems. He complains that he's "bored" without his addictions. Ang's the only one who can pilot in this terrain, leaving Spadrin with nothing much to do. Ang seems to feel it's safer to let him have what he wants. Maybe he's right; Spadrin's safer in a stupor than he is alert and restless.

This morning he walked in on me as I was using the toilet in the momentary privacy of the rover's sleeping area. He looked me up and down, smirking at my annoyance, and said, "So you impersonated a Blue. Ang was right: I'll bet you wore that uniform like you were born in it. You look like you're still wearing it—"

I pulled up my shorts. "Maybe your conscience is bothering you," I said. He laughed, but neither of us was joking, and neither of us thought it was funny. He pushed me off-balance as he went forward again.

I should have brought a weapon I could keep by me; but it would have broken the law. The law doesn't bother Spadrin. We have weapons with the supplies, but Ang keeps them locked up. The fool really thinks that makes him safe. . . .

DAY 40.

What is it about this place? It's like quicksand. . . . Time carries us forward, but the deeper we travel into World's End, the deeper I seem to sink into the past. By the time I reach Fire Lake . . .

I only wanted to get away from the campsite, and the others, for a walk this evening; another evening spent in the company of Ang and Spadrin was beginning to seem like an eternity. Number Four's immense, solitary moon was as bright as a lantern in the nearly starless sky, and the three of us could have been the only living beings on this entire world. When I set out, wandering alone in the hills seemed safer and far more pleasant than sitting at Spadrin's side.

In the moonlight the mountains looked like the weed-choked ruins of some giant's mansion, built with stones the size of houses. Like something out of the Old Empire—perhaps the cityworld of Tell'haspah, haunted by the spirits of its unremembered ancestors. The sound of the wind filled me with a homesickness for places I've never seen. I even thought of sleeping out; the cool night wind and the open sky were paradise, after the stinking closeness of the rover and Ang's snoring.

Suddenly I came upon a primitive animal trap, half hidden among the rocks and scrub in a small open space. In its jaws was something shriveled and black. I didn't know what it was until I'd gotten close enough to touch it. It was a foot, the limb of some creature that had been caught in the trap long ago. In its frenzy to live and be free, some animal had gnawed off its own foot.

I crouched there for a while, without the strength to move, before I unfastened the leather wrist guards that hid my scars. I stared at the welts on my arms. And then I opened my belt pouch and laid its contents out in the dust: the picture of my brothers, the trefoil, the picture of Song. Her hair was like the night sky, glittering blackness. Her wild dark eyes gazed into mine like the soul of this place. *I know you,* they whispered, *I know your secret heart. I know why you've come.*

I turned away from her image, to the faces of my brothers, and looked away from them. . . .

And I remembered how I had looked away from the inspector's gaze as she handed me the message transcript that had followed me to Tiamat from Kharemough.

"Sergeant," she said, more hesitantly than I'd ever heard her speak, "I'm . . . afraid it's bad news."

I felt my face go numb, and my mind. I took the transcript from her with nerveless fingers, knowing before I even looked at it what it would say. "My father is dead." I spoke the words to the naked, ancient wall of the hallway. *And I killed him.* I put out a hand to steady myself.

"I'm sorry," the inspector murmured to my turned back. And then, in her native language, she said, "May he live forever in the space of a thousand hearts."

I nodded slightly, all I could do. Finally I looked at what she had given me. The transcript was a brief, cursory message from my brother HK. It said he was now head of family, and included a copy of my father's will. I crumpled the transcript in my fist as though I could crush it out of existence. It sprang back into perfect form as I released it, and dropped to the floor. A crowd of patrolmen and rowdy offworlders pushed past us, trampling it underfoot.

"Sergeant . . ." I felt the inspector's hand fall lightly on my shoulder. I let it stay there by an effort of will. "Why don't you take the rest of the day—"

"No, Inspector." I faced her again. "I'm all right. My father— my father's been dead for more than two years." It had taken that long for the message to reach Tiamat, with the sublight time gaps at either end of the stargate. It had been years since the rituals had been spoken, years since he had joined his ancestors in the peaceful gardens. And it would be many years more before I could even think about returning to honor him there. "There's . . . nothing I can do about it now."

She frowned slightly, and said, "You can take the time to let yourself feel something." She was a tough, ironic woman— Newhavenese, like most of the force stationed there. I had been her aide for only a few months, since shortly after I arrived. She was more intelligent than most of the Newhavenese seemed to be, but until now I'd never thought of her as sensitive. I wished fiercely that she hadn't chosen this moment to demonstrate it.

"I don't want to," I whispered.

"What?"

I drew myself up. "I don't want to—to inflict my personal problems on you, Inspector. I can grieve on my own time, if that's necessary."

She glanced upward, appealing to unseen gods. Her lips moved silently, *Kharemoughis.* "Then the rest of the day is your own time," she said. "That's an order, Sergeant."

I saluted, helpless to do anything but obey. "Yes, ma'am." I started away from her. She leaned down and picked up the transcript. I stopped, turned back, holding out my hand. She gave it to me. "Thank you," I said, trying not to blink.

She smiled at me, a sad smile with a meaning I didn't really understand. "Remember the good things," she said. "Those are what last."

I nodded, but the truth was burning my throat like acid. "My father . . . loved me," I mumbled. "And I . . . I . . ." I shook my head and walked away as quickly as I could.

My father loved me. It filled my head as I went out into the teeming streets of the ancient city of Carbuncle—the jewel, the fester, that I had come so far to see. I walked the streets for hours, but I saw none of its wonders or its corruption. I saw only the past.

As I walked I remembered the exact moment when I learned that my father loved me. I was standing in the doorway to the sunroom, drawn by the rare sound of his voice raised in anger. My brothers' voices answered him, whining and resentful by turns. They were arguing about money—an argument that was far from rare.

I stood just out of sight, feeling a familiar ache in my chest at the sound of their quarrel . . . perversely aching to be a part of it. Third son, youngest by years, I had never been able to escape my birth order or my brothers' shadow; never able to matter enough to anyone to make them rage at me—

"I cannot believe thou are any sons of mine!" my father shouted. "Why can't thou behave like thy brother, with honor and wisdom! The two of thee do not make one half of him in human value."

I went to the doorway and stared into the green-dappled room. HK and SB looked up at me, and my father turned. I read the truth in all of their eyes, in a moment that seemed to go on and on.

A thousand small things that my father had done, shown me, asked of me, suddenly filled my mind—things I had ignored, always looking for something more. The walks down to the family shrine, just the two of us, on the summer evenings . . . his heirloom watch that only I had ever been allowed to hold. I thought about my brothers' endless petty torments . . . had they all sprung from jealousy?

All my life I'd felt inadequate, incomplete—only to learn, in such a way, that I was his favorite son.

Only to realize now, years too late again, that I had failed him after all. He had wanted me to stay, and I had left Kharemough. He had wanted me to . . . to change things. And I hadn't understood.

I stopped in the street, surrounded by the cacophony of shouting vendors and jostling sightseers, the shops of artisans and the garish gambling hells—a prisoner of the sights and smells and sounds, imprisoned inside the great spiral-shell of this bizarre city on an alien world. A prisoner of my own choice. I could have changed things back on Kharemough—but I had run away instead. And now it was far too late to change anything, even my mind. I had betrayed my father's belief in me . . . and his disappointment had killed him. How had it all gone so wrong? *Why didn't I understand?*

But I had. I'd known what he wanted, all along. He couldn't—wouldn't—tell me to defy the laws . . . and yet he had told me that I deserved to be his heir, which meant that he believed the laws were wrong.

I knew ways of manipulating the law. Everyone knew that there were cracks in the supposedly perfect structure of our social order. Some people—including some of our own class— actually claimed that those cracks were justifiable, even necessary, for the survival of society. But ours was an ancient family line; we had never been forced to twist tradition to prove our right to be what and where we were. Such a thing, in my father's mind, was an impossibility. I'd been raised to believe that our honor was our pride. All my life I had been taught that I was a reflection of my father, and his father, and his . . . that the way things were was the right way, the only way.

I told myself that if I tried to unseat my brothers, I would be no better than they were. And so I had left Kharemough, instead. I had followed the law; I'd believed that I had done the right thing as I had always understood it. . . . But it had only been an excuse for cowardice. Faced with the most important decision in my life, I had run away.

The rainbow streets of Carbuncle faded into the night. With a kind of disbelief, I found myself back in the future, kneeling alone on the mountainside. I stared at the scars on my wrists, at the shriveled foot of a trapped beast that I held clenched in my fist.

I put the picture of Song, the trefoil, and the desiccated stump into my belt pouch, and got to my feet.

When I returned to the campsite, Ang and Spadrin were arguing over whose turn it was to clean the dishes. Spadrin glowered and swore, but Ang's face was livid; his own anger seemed to have him by the throat. I stood silently watching them, waiting for them to come to blows over meaningless inconsequence. But Spadrin glanced up suddenly and saw me. His face spasmed as though he'd seen a ghost. And then he sent the pile of dishes clanging into the cook unit with a kick, and said, "Your turn, Gedda."

I folded my arms. "I keep the rover running. I don't do dishes."

Spadrin grunted. "You eat, don't you? If you want to go on eating, you'll do what I want."

I looked at Ang, waiting for his support. Ang wiped his arm across his mouth. He looked back at me, flexing his hands. "Who asked you to go off like that, anyway? You damn fool, I told you before we started that it was dangerous! You want to kill yourself? Don't get out of sight of the rover again, unless you don't care if you ever come back." He turned and followed Spadrin into the darkness.

I cleaned the dishes. And now I'll try to sleep—inside the rover, with the others, even though when I got here I found Spadrin sleeping in my bunk. What choice do I have . . . ?

DAY 42.

Gods, the dreams I've had. . . . If only I could remember them when I wake up; maybe they'd stop. I woke Spadrin by crying out in my sleep, before dawn; he hasn't let me forget it all day. He baits me at every turn: bumping into me when I try to meditate, spilling my tea when we eat, fouling up my equipment when I work on the rover. . . . The rough terrain we've been through has nearly torn its ancient guts out more than once. I've done all the plate-cleaning and most of the cooking, too, the past few days. It's easier than arguing about it, when Ang won't ever back me up. He never says anything to either of us that he doesn't have to, anymore. Is he more afraid of Spadrin, or his own temper?

The hell with it. I have nothing I want to say about this.

DAY 43.

Ang finally told us his plans today . . . for what it's worth.

Late this afternoon the mountains spat us out at last, and we saw the desert for the first time. The house-sized boulders sank into a pavement of perfectly hexagonal slabs of rock, blown clear of any softening dust or sand; the plain stretched away toward a distant line of powder-white hills. The sky was a cloudless indigo, and Number Four's diamond-chip sun flooded the plain with light. The silence of the day made my ears sing. The dry heat sucked the sweat from my skin as I made final repairs under the rover. It was deceptively comfortable, after the sweltering humidity we'd left behind with the jungles—but just as treacherous.

Lying on my back under the rover's jacked-up body, I heard Spadrin begin to question Ang about where we were headed next. Ang answered him in monosyllabic generalities and evasions, as usual—he hadn't given either of us any more details about his secret. But that wasn't enough for Spadrin, with the naked heart of World's End waiting for him. "Don't give me that shit," he said. "If you've got a plan, I want to know! Nobody's going to overhear us now. I want to know what we're going to find, and where it is, and how we're getting there. We're not going anyplace until I know." Ang muttered something unintelligible; then I heard a thump as someone came up hard against the side of the vehicle, making it shudder off-balance above me.

I swore and scrambled out from underneath it. As I got to my feet, I saw Ang straightening his coveralls, looking shaken. Spadrin stood watching us with a feral grin of satisfaction.

"All right," Ang said. He began to pace tensely in the small area between us. "I'll tell you what we're after. The last time I went out with a Company team, I made a discovery." He reached into a pocket and brought something out in the palm of his hand.

I looked at it, seeing only a rather nondescript egg-sized lump of stone. "What is it, some sort of ore?"

He smiled at me with an insufferable air of superiority. "It's a solii."

Spadrin slid down off the boulder. "Let me see that," he said. He snatched it from Ang's hand. "A solii? This?" He held it up to the light, but it was still only a lump of stone. "It looks like a piece of crap, to me."

"It's uncut, obviously." Ang took it back, clenching his hand.

I remembered the one or two genuine soliis I'd seen in my life . . . they seem to be on fire with their own light. It's said they were named after the legendary star Sol, the sun that first shed light on humankind, because of their transcendent beauty. There are even some cults that consider them holy; one of the stones I saw was worn by a religious mystic. "And there are more where you discovered this?" I asked.

"Yes. There are. There must be—" Ang's glance shifted. "I found it in a dry riverbed; all we have to do is track upstream until we locate the right formation, and we'll be rich . . . all of us. There'll be plenty for all of us." He looked at Spadrin as he repeated it.

"Where is it from here? How far? What are the co-ords?" Spadrin asked.

Ang just looked at him.

Spadrin spat an iesta pod. "Listen, dirteater, you called this a partnership. I want my share of everything, and that means all you know. You can tell me now, or you can tell me the hard way." He flexed his hands.

"Ang," I muttered, "if you tell him that, you've got nothing—"

Ang only shrugged, moving away from me. He said, to Spadrin, "It's a few days' travel southeast from here to the place where I found the solii. I don't know how far we'll have to go from there to find the formation. Any co-ords I could give you would be meaningless, anyway. Normal readings are useless. I navigate by landmark and experience. . . . Sometimes even that doesn't work. Things *change* out here, you understand? Every time I go out, I see things twisted around. You've got to know World's End, or you won't survive. I'm the only one who can find what we want. And I'm the only one who can get us out again. Don't ever forget it." He searched our faces, to be sure we believed him. Spadrin spat out another pod, but he nodded.

"Why are you doing this?" I asked. "Why didn't you follow up on this before, when you first found the solii?"

He laughed once; the sound was more like a curse. "Because if I'd reported it, all the profits would belong to the Company. So I quit. Even splitting what we find with them and you, I'll be rich. This is my reward. No one can take it away from me. No one." The hand that held the solii made a fist. He asked me, "Are you finished yet?"

I shook my head. "Soon. But we'd better have easier terrain from here on, or I don't know how long I'll be able to keep this wreck moving."

He glared at me. "We'll make it." He turned away.

"Ang?" I called, and he looked back. "How close will we come to Fire Lake?"

He shrugged. "Too close for comfort. The closer you get to Fire Lake, the crazier everything gets."

"How likely are we to meet anyone else out here?"

He shrugged again. "You never know. And you don't want to know the ones who are glad to see you. . . . Why?"

"I just wondered," I answered lamely. To even try to explain my real reason for being here at this point seemed absurd. Ang walked away from the rover, away from us. I felt a kind of helpless fatalism settle over me as I watched him go, looking out into the wasteland. World's End was far vaster and more desolate than I had ever imagined. And yet I had to reach Fire Lake, and I needed Ang to do it. I tried to tell myself that once we found his treasure, I could convince the others to search for my brothers in return for my share. . . . I tried not to wonder what would happen if my share actually made me rich enough to buy back the family estates myself.

I started to climb into the rover's cab to take some readings, but Spadrin caught my arm, jerking me back and around.

"What are you really here for? It isn't to get rich." His hand probed the tendons of my elbow and found a nerve.

I gasped and swore. "Damn you! I told you never to touch me—" My voice slid away from me.

"Or what?" Spadrin blocked my escape with his outstretched arm. "You'll report me? You'll have me arrested? Who's going to back you up? I'll tell you who." He grinned. "No one, Blue. No one." He stepped back, letting his arm drop. "It doesn't matter why you're here, right now. When I really want to know, you'll tell me; just like Ang. *Gedda.*" He spoke the word very softly, deliberately, before he walked away.

I sat down on the step of the cab. I sat there for a long time, staring at the desolation that surrounded me. But my eyes saw snow, not stones, and a circle of pale-faced barbarians with eyes the color of the sky. Tiamat's sky; Tiamat's people—the outlaws who had taken a police inspector captive in the frozen wilderness outside Carbuncle, who had degraded and tortured him. . . . The one called Taryd Roh, who had taught their prisoner that pride was no defense against pain; who knew how to use his hands the way Spadrin did. He had used them on a man trapped like an animal in a cage . . . a man who had begged, who had wept, who had crawled to please him . . . who would have done anything he asked. Anything. But he didn't want anything.

Afterward, the prisoner had taken the lid of a food can and slashed his own wrists.

Death before dishonor. We drank the blood toast when I was in school, and laughed. Suicide before shame: the code of our ancestors, a testament to our integrity. We could laugh then. We were so young . . . so sure that none of us would ever know suffering or humiliation, never see our humanity stripped naked, or our honor ground into the dirt. . . .

"Gedda? Gedda!" I looked up, into Ang's scowling face and the glare of the sun behind him. I shielded my eyes, trying to hide my confusion.

"Something wrong?" He was staring at me.

I shook my head. "No. No, I . . ." I realized suddenly that my eyes were wet. I rubbed them with my hand. "I got grit in my eye. Had to get it out—" I groped for the canteen behind me.

"You finished?"

"No, goddamn it! Leave me alone, let me do my job!"

He grunted and walked away again. I opened the canteen and gulped water, spilling it down the front of my shirt; wasting it, not caring. It eased the knotted tightness inside me, letting me breathe, letting me find the self-discipline to concentrate on my work again.

I wanted to die, on Tiamat. I should have died—but I didn't. Gods, was I really spared by fate for this?

DAY 45.

Ang is leading us on a crazy chase. Sometimes I wonder, does he really know where we're going? If he does, then he must be trying to make sure we can't get back without him. He still does virtually all the piloting, when he can't point one of us at some distant landmark and tell us to aim for it. He won't give us any bearings.

We've long since left the mountains behind, and the plain of stones. The rover continues to carry us along, the gods know how; running on instinct, like Ang, maybe. I hold my breath every morning. My hands are raw with cuts and blisters from the repair work; sometimes I can barely handle my tools.

We've crossed long-dead sea floor, crushing the skeleton shells of a million tiny nameless creatures; floundered through mineral deposits like new-fallen snow, beds the Company hasn't even begun to think about exploiting . . . seen pillars of salt and potash wind-sculpted into the forms of agonized victims. . . .

Last night I dreamed that I was journeying through the purity of the winter wilderness with Moon; that I was free in a

way that I had never been free, from the past, from the future . . .
until I saw stars falling into a sea of light beyond the snow-
covered ridges; and the snow became desert, and I dreamed
that I had turned to salt. I wanted to weep, but my tears were a
salty crust, filling my eyes until I was blind. I tried to scream,
but my voice had turned to crystals. I tasted salt, and when I
woke my mouth was bleeding; I'd bitten my tongue.

I remember my nightmares, now. I began to remember them
the day Spadrin—the day we left the mountains. The worst ones
are about *her*. Because I can only bring her back to me by looking
into the face of death. . . .

The prisoner of my nightmares dreams of falling, spiraling
down, down—the patrolcraft knocked out of the sky by a stolen
beamer in the hands of the outlaw nomads he was pursuing.
White terror paralyzes him again as an old hag raises her gun
to kill him . . . and then she lowers it, and suddenly he realizes
that they will not even let him die honorably. They are going to
force him to live, as their slave. In that moment he wishes
he had died, because in that moment his world has ended.

But he lives on, a living death in a squalid, windowless, hopeless room of stone, caged with a menagerie of wretched, stinking animals. Days bleed into weeks and months, and he becomes
a human animal, hungry, filthy, freezing. Savages the lowest-
born Kharemoughi would not even call human humiliate
and harass him, leaving him with nothing—not privacy, not
decency, not even shame. He tries to escape, and fails. For punishment he is given to Taryd Roh, whose pleasure is creating
pain. And then he is left alone, in such agony that he cannot
move, to ask the unforgiving silence *Why?* Why has this happened to him? All his life he has been told that virtue is rewarded, all his life he has tried to do what was right . . . but

now, lying in his own blood and vomit, he looks back over his life and sees only failure: his mother's leaving, his father's death, his brothers' mocking faces. Without honor, without hope, all that he has left is a black hunger for death.

And so, when he can find the strength to move again, he takes the lid of a can and opens his veins *(as his mother disappears into the colors of dawn)*, but the girl who keeps the animals finds him too soon. He refuses to eat or drink *(as incense rises into the clear air above his father's tomb)*, until Taryd Roh brings him a meal. He runs out into the heart of a blizzard when they forget to watch him *(believing that the Change is past, that his own people have left Tiamat forever; wanting only to die a free man)*, only to wander in circles in the storm and be recaptured. . . .

Delirious with sickness and fever, he lies in the arms of Death; and her face is the Child Stealer's, as fair as aurora-glow—a ghost out of boyhood nursery tales, a changer of souls. She smiles and makes him drink strange herbal brews; she promises him that soon . . . She grants him sleep.

But he wakes again, to find the Child Stealer wearing the grieving, weary face of another prisoner, whose name is Moon. She is a Tiamatan, and when his mind is clear enough to think at all, he feels only suspicion and anger. But she speaks to him in his own language, telling him news of his home; she heals him with a sibyl's skills and a gentleness he can scarcely believe. He begins to trust her, as she forces him to remember that a universe still exists somewhere beyond the frozen fields of hell.

He watches Moon in Transfer, and feels the awe that even the nomads feel to see her control powers no ordinary human could endure. And he begins to realize the greater power that is hers—the strength of her spirit, which lets her accept and endure and still struggle to change what he knows is hopeless.

Despair has become a prison deeper than the cave of stone for him; but every day she makes him admit that, at least for this day, he can bear to go on living. She tells him stories to make him laugh; she tells him the Hegemony is unjust, to make him react. She helps him repair a piece of the stolen equipment that the nomads bring to him; and it is not her hands working alongside his own, but her calm belief in his competence that makes him succeed.

And she tells him about the lover who left her when she became a sibyl; how she has searched for him ever since, even though she knows he loves someone else—Arienrhod, the ageless, corrupt queen of Winter. Moon's clone, her own mother, her opposition in a game of fate played out by the unpredictable, omniscient sibyl machinery. . . . But she knows nothing of that, now. She only knows that her obsession has brought her to this place; just as his own failures have brought him here.

She asks him, finally, about the half-healed wounds on his wrists. But when he tells her what they mean, he sees nothing in her eyes except a profound knowledge of shared pain. He realizes with a kind of wonder that to her he is not his father's son. He is not a highborn Kharemoughi disgraced beyond enduring. He is not a failed suicide, a weakling, a coward. Reflected in her eyes at last he sees the man he has always longed to be . . . a quiet, intelligent, capable man, a man who serves the law, a man who has shown her only gentleness and respect. An honorable man.

She believes in him; she believes the future that her sibyl visions have shown to her still exists, for both of them. And suddenly all that matters to him is that he is no longer alone. He takes her into his arms, holding her briefly, chastely, only for a moment; filled with a gratitude too profound for words.

And as he tries to let her go, she clings to him, murmuring, "No, not yet. Hold me, just for now. . . ."

He is afraid, as suddenly he knows that he was afraid all along, that if he felt her body so close to him he would never let her go. But he takes her in his arms again, sheltering her, answering her need; knowing all the while that it is another man's arms she longs to feel around her.

And as he realizes that even his love is hopeless, he realizes how much he loves her, has always loved her, will love her until he dies. The code that controls his life, that has told him his life is no longer worth living, would have forbidden this love he feels for a barbarian girl as pale as moonlight. . . . But her reality makes his Truth as transparent as a lie; she makes his scars invisible. His arms tighten around her; bittersweet longing and desire are all he knows, and all he needs to know.

With a kind of amazement he feels her heartbeat quicken, answering his own. . . .

And then it ends. It always ends. Because it was never real, goddamn it! It was always a dream—even while it was happening. It could never have lasted. Her life was becoming a part of history, and I was nothing but a footnote. I knew it then, in my mind if not my heart. That's why I left her. . . .

Then, why did leaving Tiamat leave me so empty—?

And when she disappears, why does it leave me so afraid?

The fear spills over into the daytime, until I have to blink my eyes to separate salt and sand from snow. . . . Spadrin's eyes are *not* the color of the sky. Ang's eyes are as black as jet, and as impenetrable. Are we his partners, or his pawns? What really goes on in his mind? How could he have spent so long out here, and not have been affected somehow by this place . . . ? He eats and sleeps and stares off into the distance with his lenses as if he's alone.

Song's eyes stare into my soul, night after night. . . . A sibyl found me once, in the wilderness, and saved me. And now a sibyl calls to me, *Come to Fire Lake . . . find me . . . save me.* Save me—

I . . . What the hell am I saying? I'm tired. . . . I'm just tired, that's all.

Where are my brothers, goddamn them . . . ? What did I do with their picture?

DAY 48.

Spadrin did it intentionally. I know he did. He told Ang it was an accident, and Ang pretends to believe him . . . what else? But I know they're both liars.

I had to work on the rover again today, a little past noon. Something had ripped or come loose underneath the vehicle, and the cab began to overheat. Before long it was worse inside the rover than outside. We had to stop; I had to work on it.

We were passing the foot of a scarp at the time. We all got out; Spadrin and Ang headed for the narrow strip of shade below the cliff face. They slipped and clattered through piles of what I thought was detritus from the slope. But when I followed, I found the piles were really heaps of bleached bones. I looked up the face of the scarp; its rim was like the serrated edge of a knife against the sky, fifty meters above our heads. "Ang?" I asked. "What happened here? These bones . . ." I'd scarcely seen a living creature larger than an insect since we'd left the mountains. Ang had said most desert creatures were nocturnal, but I could as easily believe they were simply nonexistent.

Ang settled on an outcrop of sandstone, picking desultorily through the bones with something that might have been a femur. The bones seemed to be from a lot of different species. I wondered how long it had taken for such a monument of death to accumulate here. He shrugged. "Sometimes it happens out here. Things just go crazy—throw themselves off a cliff, run themselves to death; whole mobs of them. There are other boneyards like this. . . . This one used to be farther north." He shrugged again, as if living in a topologist's nightmare was perfectly natural.

"Why?" I said. "Why do they go mad?" Even as I asked, I thought that maybe he'd already answered me.

"Nobody knows why. Nobody cares, except the bugs." He pointed with his jaw, and I saw the line of half-meter hummocks that lay baking like loaves of bread in the sun near the rover. Deathwatch beetles—carrion eaters, the funeral attendants of the waste. Ang had said they gather around a dying creature, waiting until it's helpless, but not necessarily dead. . . . *Like Spadrin,* I thought.

Spadrin was kicking a clear space in the shade with noisy disgust. He sat down, opening a bottle of liquor, and squinted up at me. "Get to work, Tech. It's hot out here."

I put on my sun helmet and took a long drink of water. Then I went back to the rover and crawled under its front end, shouldering bones and rocks out of my way. The rover's body absorbed the desert heat and reradiated it. My shirt was soaked with perspiration immediately, and my head began to throb. I hoped I could finish the repairs before I passed out.

Spadrin turned on his receiver; it was picking up some entertainment broadcast on inescapable satellite feed all the way from Foursgate. Strident, insipid music rolled incongruously from the scarp and evaporated into the silence of the desert. Minutes passed like days, but at last I was able to patch the gutted cooling system back together. "Ang," I called, "check the cab, will you? Turn on the cooler."

I heard someone come to the rover and climb into the cab. After another interminable wait, a pair of desert boots stepped down again into the dust. "It's working," Spadrin's voice said grudgingly. "Took you long enough."

I began to push myself out from under the rover as he stalked back toward the shade. And that was when he did it. As he passed the nearest beetle mound he kicked it, deliberately, caving in its brittle wall.

A stream of sky-colored beetles poured out through the breach. Before I could get to my feet they were swarming all over me, in my clothes, my hair, my mouth—

I don't remember clearly what happened after that; except that somehow I found myself naked and reeking of alcohol, bleeding from a hundred tiny, smarting gouges all over my body. Ang stood in front of me, holding a bottle of Spadrin's liquor. He shoved the bottle into my mouth and forced me to take a drink. I coughed and spat it out, struggling to get away from him. I leaned down, groping for my clothes, furious with humiliation. My clothing was soaked and caked with alcoholic mud; more bottles—empty ones—lay scattered in the dirt. The beetles were gone. I struggled with my underwear.

"Don't hurry on my account," Ang said sardonically. "I'd shake everything twice, if I was you."

I turned my back on him and shook everything out again with clumsy hands. I picked an opalescent blue-green beetle out of my shirt pocket. After that my body did most of the shaking for me.

"Relax," Ang said. "It's over. At least you got the shower you've been bitching about." I stared at him, incredulous. He was smiling, but I couldn't tell what he meant by it.

Spadrin climbed down out of the rover's cab. He looked sullenly at the ring of bottles, at me, and at Ang. "That's half of what I had left."

Ang shrugged. "Only way to get rid of the bugs. You're the one who . . . tripped." His voice was flat.

Spadrin didn't answer him. "Got all the cooties out, Gedda?" He looked at me instead, and I knew exactly what lay behind his smile.

"You did that intentionally—"

"Me? How did I know they'd come out of there like that?"

"You knew!"

"You want to make something of it?" His smile stretched taut. He flexed his hands almost casually. "Gedda—?"

My own hands made fists. They loosened again. I looked down at my naked legs, away from his eyes, and shook my head. The hot breath of the desert whispered around me, stinging me with dust.

"Then say thanks for wasting my supply." He glanced at the empty bottles.

I looked up again, felt my face flushing.

"Forget it," Ang murmured, to someone, to the wind. "Just forget about it. . . ."

Spadrin stood where he was, waiting.

Anger paralyzed my throat. I tried, once, twice, before I could get the word out. "Thanks."

Spadrin climbed back inside, and let us follow.

DAY 49.

At least I think it's day 49. My watch isn't keeping time—even its logic functions are off. The cooling unit isn't in much better condition. Neither am I. Neither are the others, I suppose, but I don't give a damn. It's the middle of the night, and the inside of the rover is barely cool even now. I did the best I could. I can't do it all alone, without parts, without help. . . . That's what they expect. Miracles. In this stinking place?

Gods, how I want to go outside, breathe fresh air, even if it has to be here— But Ang claims it's too dangerous to leave the vehicle at night; that we might lose our way, or . . . or what, he won't say. Step on a beetle hive.

I feel those bugs crawling on me, all the time; I can't rest. I itch all over, my eyes water, I start shaking. . . . Ang says I'm having an allergic reaction. Spadrin grins as if he planned it that way. Ang gave me salves and some kind of antihistamine, or I'd have crawled out of my skin by now. Every bite is oozing and swollen; they stick to my clothes; I can't stand touching them but I have to scratch. . . . I hate Spadrin. . . . Gods, I have to stop thinking about it!

DAY 54.
DAY 55?

The only thing I really know for sure is that we finally reached the place where Ang found the solii. It was a couple of mornings ago; I was spelling Ang at the controls, to keep from going crazy with itching. It was almost midday when I began to see a line of hills ahead. Clouds of mist lay in their folds, like lint in pockets. To see fog lying on the land was more than my eyes could believe—after so many days in World's End, I thought it was a hallucination. I was still waiting for it to disappear when Ang came stumbling forward, with a reeking fesh stick in his hand. I turned as I heard him, and saw his eyes widen as he looked through the windshield. He was excited; it was the first time since we began this journey that I remembered seeing any positive emotion on his face. Then he turned back and swore at me. "Why the hell didn't you call me?"

"I thought it wasn't real," I said, scratching at a scab.

"It's real." He nodded, and wiped sweat from his eyes. "It's real, all right. This is what we've been looking for." He sounded relieved. He gestured me up from my seat and took the controls.

As we drew closer I began to make out foliage on the hills. The spiny fireshrub and stunted thorn trees weren't much, but they were better than the last plant life I remembered—the bloated, unwholesome flora of the jungle. I strained for the first glimpse of the blue-water lake my imagination had set deep in some twisting valley.

But as we entered the hills, in the blaze of noon, the mists still clung unnaturally to the land ahead of us. Looking past Ang's shoulder, I asked, "What's up there in that fog?"

"Hellfire and brimstone," he said, with a bark of laughter. "Geothermal area." We entered the wall of fog.

The temperature fell unexpectedly as we traveled deeper into the hills. Clouds of sulphurous mist poured from craters large enough to swallow the rover whole. Their rims were stained with minerals—ochres of yellow and red, greens, whites. The anemic gray ground we passed over breathed fog; droplets of condensation glistened on leaves and branches, and splattered our windshield.

Eventually, after hours of silent journeying, we reached a vast, shallow lake—but not the lake I'd imagined. Its steaming surface was perfectly transparent, but mineral springs tinted its depths with delicate pinks and blues, like blossoms under glass. Ang stopped the rover on the shore and said, "There's a geyser somewhere around here. Goes off about once a day. I need it to give me a bearing on the place where I found the solii. We'll camp here tonight, find it tomorrow."

"Here?" Spadrin said, and swore. He'd come forward finally, and the view through the dome was enough to startle him out of his plughead stupor. I'd watched him grow more and more uneasy as we entered this place. He's obviously never been so intimate before with the unpleasant reality of a planet's surface. "I don't like it here."

"What's the matter?" I said. "Is hell too close for comfort?"

He swore at me, this time, and I saw a faint smile pull up the corner of Ang's mouth. I let myself smile, for the first time in days, but only after Spadrin turned away.

"What the—?" Spadrin's back muscles bunched as he looked out at the steaming lake again. "Ang! What the hell is that?"

Ang leaned forward in his seat; so did I. A line of figures was coming toward us through the mist along the lake shore. They moved with the slow, jerky progress of thorn trees come to life. My mind tried to make their shapes human, and failed. I echoed Spadrin: "What are those?"

Ang pushed eagerly up out of his seat. "Cloud ears, by the gods! Cloud ears." They gathered around the rover in a crowd of disordered limbs. As they peered in, Ang reached for the door-release.

Spadrin gripped his arm, jerking him away. "You're not letting those *things* in here!"

Ang pulled free. "You think I'm a fool? They're harmless. . . . I'm going out to them."

"Why?" Spadrin said.

"They pick things up."

"There's a man out there too," I said. My eyes had finally found a human form among the stalklike limbs and bulbous glittering eyes.

Ang looked up and out again. He started to frown, and then he pushed past Spadrin and disappeared into the back of the rover. When he came forward again he had three stun rifles. He handed us each one. "You know how to use these?"

Spadrin laughed. I nodded once.

The feel of the gun in my hand was like water in the throat of a man dying of thirst. I weighed its balance, checked the charge almost automatically. When I looked up again, Spadrin was watching me. Ang opened the door.

As we climbed down from the cab the natives shuffled back with the sound of dry branches clattering. There were maybe a dozen of them, and they were larger than I'd expected— probably taller than an average human if they stood upright. They hunched over, resting on long, fragile arms that looked like bones wrapped in bark. I had the sudden peculiar thought that the arms should have been wings. They did have fingers, spindly twigs that were constantly sifting the crusty soil, picking things up for brief scrutiny and dropping them again. An unreadable proboscis of wrinkled gray-brown was all the face I could make out on any of them. They wore clothing after a fashion—filthy rags hard to distinguish from their desiccated flesh, and an assortment of small bags and pouches that hung against their chests. The human who stood among them wore rags, too, and carried pouches and a gnarled staff. If he wanted to look like one of them, he was succeeding. Why in the name of a thousand gods he would, I couldn't begin to imagine.

The natives came forward again as Ang made a motion; the human moved with them. Ang had dropped a sack of his own on the ground and pulled it open, never taking his eyes off of them. The sack was full of bits of broken equipment, spools of wire, globs of melted glass. There were stones also, bright and peculiar ones, probably every bit as worthless as the rest of it.

At the sight of Ang's pile, the cloud ears set up an eerie, high-pitched trilling that made my skin crawl. I watched their twig-fingers reaching for their pouches, quivering with anticipation.

"Wait! Wait!" the human cried suddenly, throwing back the folds of his cloak.

"A woman!" Spadrin muttered, at the sight that was abruptly obvious to us all. A woman well into middle age, with a face and a half-naked body as wrinkled and weather-beaten as any native's.

She struck left and right with her staff, driving the cloud ears into squealing confusion. "Not yet, not yet!"

Ang held up his rifle, pointing it at her. "What the hell are you doing?" It wasn't one of the questions I would have asked, but it was sufficient to get her attention. She cocked her head at us, as if she'd suddenly registered us as sentient. She wrapped her cloak around her, clothing herself in unexpected dignity as she stepped forward. "Are you here to exploit these unfortunate savages, as all your ancestors have done since time before remembering?" The cloud ears shuffled and trilled behind her like a flock of impatient customers. But they waited.

Ang gaped at her for a long moment. Finally he lowered his gun and said, "No."

She seemed to seriously consider that. "Then I bless this congregation of fate with the presence of the Sacred Aurant." She mumbled some more words in a sublanguage I didn't know, and lowered her staff in turn. The natives rushed past her and began to pick through Ang's offerings. She smiled benignly, making chirrups and whistles that sounded like their speech.

"Who is she?" I murmured to Ang.

He shrugged. "How would I know?"

"What's the Aurant?" Spadrin asked.

"The Fellowship of the Divine Aurant has a cathedral in Foursgate," I said. "I thought it was a well-respected order."

"It is." Ang nodded. He reached absently to touch the religious medal he wore. The natives were picking over his stones and pieces, putting ones they fancied into their bags and pouches. And in return, things from their hoards were appearing on the ground beside his sack. "The Fellowship does a lot of missionary work. . . ." Ang said. Spadrin laughed abruptly. Ang glared at him.

The woman was studying us from beyond the pile of trade goods. "Are you with the Fellowship?" I called, not really ready to believe that their missionaries were forced to endure such extremes of deprivation.

Her eyes brightened, and she came toward us. "Are you true believers?"

Spadrin laughed again, sourly, and Ang shrugged.

I nodded, not wanting to get involved in a discussion about it. "Are you all right out here?"

"Of course!" She looked at me as if I'd asked something absurd. "I've come to guide these poor unfortunates into the light of true knowledge, out of the darkness of their wretched solitude."

I kept my face expressionless, wondering why religious fanatics always sounded so florid, and so much alike. I noticed that her feet shuffled constantly in the dirt. As I watched, she picked up a stone with her bare toes and put it into her hand. She glanced at it, tossed it away, began her restless shuffling again. My hands tightened over my equipment belt. "How long have you been out here . . . uh, doing missionary work?"

"Oh, many years, many years of your time—" She waved a

hand as if she were sweeping time aside. "The Aurant's work is never done. It is a constant struggle to keep these poor unfortunates from backsliding into their former degraded ways. They've come so far along the road to understanding!" Another wave of her hand.

I looked past her at the cloud ears, their frantic jostle for position beginning to ease as they finished picking over Ang's junk. I scratched my shoulder, wondering bleakly what they must have been like before. She turned with me to watch them, and then she drifted away toward the pile. She kneeled down among them and began to pick over their leavings: choosing, discarding, replacing.

"She's a fucking shufflebrain," Spadrin muttered. But his eyes stayed on her.

Ang folded his arms, like a man afraid of contamination.

"If she's been with them for years, why haven't you ever seen her before?" I asked.

Ang rubbed at his beard. "Who the hell knows? Maybe she just thinks it's been years. Or maybe these aren't the same natives. They all look alike to me. They wander all over World's End. Funny thing, there aren't supposed to be that many, but I see them all the time."

"Are these any better off than the rest?"

He raised his eyebrows. "Better off?" He shook his head. "No."

I grimaced. The cloud ears were fading into the mist, as abruptly as they'd appeared. The woman got to her feet, putting a last bright flake of glass into the pouch hanging from her neck. She looked at us intently, and said, "What you seek does not exist; it is all an illusion." For a moment I felt a chill, thinking that somehow she knew our very thoughts. "Only the soul can perceive the true nature of time. Ask the Aurant to guide you to knowledge."

My neck muscles loosened as I realized she was only preaching nonsense again.

But Spadrin followed her as she began to shuffle away. He said, unexpectedly, "I want to hear more about the Aurant."

I watched them go, uneasily, knowing that Spadrin was capable of anything but finding religion. I started after them—and stumbled over Ang, who had crouched down to collect his offerings, completely oblivious to everything else.

He swore, straightening up, with his fists full of the natives' leavings. "Watch where you're going, for the love of the Aurant!" The oath hung self-consciously between us.

"Sorry." I bobbed my head. He was sorting and discarding bits of stone even while he swore. I realized that the natives must pick up things of value as well as rubbish in their wanderings, and that they were just as likely to leave him those things in return for his bright trash as they were to leave something worthless. "Did you get your money's worth?"

He frowned at the sarcasm. "Not yet." He kept on sorting; held something up with an exclamation, and put it into the pocket of his coveralls. He glanced at me again, defensive. "They get what they want, and so do—"

Someone screamed.

"What—?" Ang said.

"Spadrin!" I left him and ran along the lake shore in the direction Spadrin and the woman had taken. I broke through the wall of mist into a clear space; found the woman lying on the ground with blood bright on her face and her rags of clothing half torn away. Spadrin was on top of her. Without thinking I grabbed the collar of his jacket. I dragged him off of her and shoved him away, hit him with my fist. He landed in a thicket of fireshrub.

I turned back to help the woman, but suddenly there was another scream, behind me. This time it was Spadrin. I saw him struggling in the thicket. And then I saw what had made him scream—the undulating bag of flesh that clung to his leg with barbed tentacles. Blood streamed down his boot.

"Gedda!" he shouted frantically. "Shoot it! Stun it, kill it, get it off me!"

I lifted my stun rifle. But then I looked over my shoulder at the woman struggling up onto her knees, mumbling incoherencies, while two of the cloud ears buzzed solicitously around her.

"Gedda!" Spadrin shrieked. I looked back at him again, at the white terror on his face. I aimed the gun, had the bloodwart clearly in its sights. But still I didn't fire.

Suddenly Ang was beside me. He lifted his weapon and fired without hesitation. The creature squealed and went limp, but it didn't drop from Spadrin's spastically kicking leg. Ang went forward to kneel at Spadrin's side, pinning down his leg. "Give me your knife." Spadrin gave it to him, and Ang began to pry at the creature's pincer mouth still embedded in Spadrin's flesh.

"What—what *is* that?" Spadrin gasped.

"Bloodwart," Ang said expressionlessly. "Big one." The mouth came free, and blood gushed from the wound.

I looked away, and saw the silent ring of natives standing just far enough back to be almost lost in the fog. Watching. I had the feeling they'd been watching all along. I turned and went to where the woman stood plucking absently at her rags, chirruping to the natives beside her. "Are you all right?" I asked.

She looked at me, jerking like a puppet, stark fear on her face. It faded into wariness as she saw that I was not Spadrin.

"I'm sorry," I said, suddenly ashamed for my entire sex. "Spadrin is an animal, not a man. He won't harm you again. I'm a police inspector—" Saying it just to reassure her.

She bent her head, looking at me sideways. "A police inspector?"

I nodded. I slung my rifle over my shoulder and approached her slowly, hands open. "Did he hurt you badly?" The blood on her face seemed to be nothing more serious than a cut lip.

"No, no, I'm all right," she said, too briskly, shaking her head and wiping at her mouth. "I'm quite all right, Inspector. The Aurant protects me, I can come to no harm."

I hesitated, not certain whether her glazed expression was fanaticism or simply shock; not wanting to push her over the edge of control, either way.

"You must arrest that poor unfortunate, Inspector. You must put him in a small white room with no day or night and instruct him in the teachings of the Aurant until he has seen the true nature of time. You must do that with all your prisoners, and when they understand, there will be no more need for prisons, for the Millennium will have come."

I cleared my throat, glancing away at the watching cloud ears. More of them had gathered around us; their shuffling dance whispered through my nerves. "Where did the bloodwart come from?" I asked it more of them than of her.

"From the Aurant," she said, a little impatiently. "All things may be found in all places, if only you know how to see. These creatures of the spirit know it far better than you ever will."

I shook my head, resigned. "The three of us will be gone from this place by tomorrow, at least," I said. I wondered how much of anything I said she really understood. "Until then—"

"Tomorrow?" She scattered time with a wave of her hands. "Who knows where any of us will be tomorrow?"

"Are you . . . do you need any more help? Is there anything that I can do for you, anything at all?" Guilt made me ask, and ask again.

She merely laughed. She said, as if she were sharing a secret, "I have the true understanding. I need nothing more." She whistled to the natives and began to shuffle away. It was clear that what had happened five minutes past had already left her mind.

I shrugged and started back to the rover. A part of me argued that she should be returned to civilization and helped somehow. But she seemed happy where she was, thinking she understood some hidden truth. Who am I to interfere—I, who understand less and less.

When I got back to the rover Ang was finishing up the bandage on Spadrin's wound. They both looked up at me, Ang's expression unreadable, as usual, and Spadrin's murderous.

"Is she all right?" Ang asked, with what sounded like genuine concern.

I nodded. "As all right as she could be. He didn't have a chance to really harm her."

Ang nodded in turn and picked up the medical supplies. "Don't try to go anywhere on that leg." He shot a warning glance at Spadrin and climbed into the vehicle's cab.

"You fucking son of a bitch," Spadrin hissed at me when Ang was out of earshot. His face was a map of red scratches from the fireshrub, and a bruise was forming on his jaw where I hit him. "You think I don't know why you didn't shoot? You wanted that bloodsucker to drain me dry!"

"And you tried to rape that woman!"

"A crazy woman—"

"What the hell difference does that make? You degenerate, the thought of breathing the same air you breathe makes me sick. I know your type—"

"And I know yours." He leaned forward, baring his teeth at me. "*Gedda.* I know what that means on your homeworld, Tech. It means failed suicide—coward. That's what those scars mean too. They mean you're dead to your own people, even if you didn't have the guts to end it all like a real man. What did you do that they found out about? What's really wrong with you? You don't like it with women; maybe you like it with men? Or with something—"

I caught him by the front of his jacket, dragging him to his feet.

It was just what he wanted. Suddenly I was sprawled on the ground; all his weight was on top of me, and the blade of his knife hovered over my eyes. I cursed myself with helpless fury.

"You thought you were smarter than us, didn't you, Gedda? Well, now you see just how much you really know about anything." He spat the words into my face. I flinched, and he laughed.

"Ang!" I shouted, bit it off as the knife lowered.

"Shut up." His free hand caught my chin. "You answer what I ask, and that's all. Understand?"

I nodded, panting. "What—what do you want to know?"

His mouth pulled back in an ugly smile, and the blade brushed my lashes.

I shut my eyes, trying to turn my face away. "What? What? *Please—*"

The pressure lifted slowly from my eyelids. "You've just told me everything I needed to know."

I opened my eyes, blinking them back into focus.

His hand moved suddenly, swiftly, and pain blazed above my eyes.

I heaved him off of me with a strength born of sheer fright. He scrambled to his feet, standing over me before I could get my body under control again. Looking up and past him, I saw Ang's face behind the darkened dome of the cab—looking out, watching everything that happened. When my eyes found his, his face disappeared from view.

Spadrin glanced over his shoulder, following my gaze. He looked back at me, and he began to laugh again. His laughter was almost like sobbing. He was still laughing as he climbed heavily into the rover's cab.

I lay where I'd fallen. The wound on my forehead was like a burning-glass, a focus for all the pain in the world. Finally, when I could make myself move again, I got to my feet. I looked at my reflection in the shadowy mirror of the dome. A bloody S marked my forehead; a trickle of red crept down the bridge of my nose as I watched. Spadrin had cut his initial into my flesh— like a brand, a mark of ownership.

I covered my forehead with my hand and turned away. The thought of getting back into the rover, of facing either Spadrin or Ang, was more than I could stand. I moved away along the shore, stumbling like a drunkard, until I reached the spot where Spadrin had attacked the missionary. There was no sign of the woman or the cloud ears—no sign that any living thing had ever been there.

I actually wondered for a moment if it had really happened. I wiped blood from my face, rubbed the sticky redness between my fingers, staring at it. I sat down in the sand. *He knows why I'm here.* I swore softly. Did I really say to that woman,

He won't harm you, I'm a police inspector? A police inspector! A liar, and a hypocrite. Once my uniform was a suit of armor. But there was no one inside it after I left Tiamat. Damn Tiamat! I lost everything there, my honor, my heart . . .

My innocence. I could live without honor—even without a heart—as long as I could go on doing my duty. Being usefully alive, not staining anyone else with the poison of my shame. But I couldn't even do that, after I left Tiamat . . . because I no longer believed in the perfection of the law.

On Tiamat I served in the Hegemonic Police, suppressing an entire world's economic progress so that the Hegemony could go on running it in absentia. And the only reason it even mattered was the water of life—an obscene luxury that required the slaughter of thousands of helpless creatures . . . creatures some people even claimed were intelligent beings. I helped to persecute sibyls, denying their wisdom to a world that had as much right to it as we ever did, and far more need of it—because any Tiamatan who learned that the real source of the sibyls' wisdom was not their Goddess but a data bank could use it against us. I helped the Hegemony maintain its control through ignorance and lies, and believed that I was honorable.

But then I found Moon—or she found me, and made me love her; and I saw my uniform through my lover's eyes. I saw the monstrous hypocrisy that I had called justice, and couldn't look away.

When I met her she was proscribed, simply because she had been offworld—a right only Tiamatans were denied. She had learned a sibyl's real power; and the sibyl machinery itself willed her to use it to end our tyranny of ignorance. But simply by knowing the truth about her gift, and wanting to use it fully, she broke our laws. . . . She saved my life; but if I had done my duty she would have been exiled for it. I could have had her put into my charge, taken her offworld with me, even forced her to marry me.

But instead I lied and evaded and broke half a dozen laws myself to get her safely into Carbuncle, so that she could follow the destiny the sibyl mind had forced upon her.

And then I left Tiamat without her, and without denouncing her, even though the sibyl mind had made her queen. I left her to her lover, even though he was a corrupt weakling; even though I knew that she would forget me, and do everything she could to teach her world to hate my own. Because I believed that it was right, because I knew that a power greater and far wiser than the Hegemony meant it to happen that way. And because I . . . because I loved her. I left Tiamat a queen who could give her people a real future; but I left Tiamat as a traitor to my own people, and to myself. I was even proud of it. I felt like a saint, like the bearer of some secret truth. . . .

Like a love-blind fool, like a coward. There is no truth; there are only differences of opinion.

But I came to Number Four, and tried to say that it was all behind me, forgotten, an aberration; tried to get on with my duty and my life. I memorized every law on record, and enforced them to the letter! But now all I could see was that I was living a lie, going through motions that hid the emptiness inside the form, like a saint without a god. Until my brothers came, and told me what I'd—what they'd done. The final failure of the law. And after that even self-discipline wasn't enough to save me.

It was only a matter of time before I ended up here. Did everyone see it but me—?

I sat by the steaming lake until darkness fell. I tried to meditate, alone in the susurrous twilight, but I couldn't concentrate on even the simplest adhani. I couldn't face returning to the rover, either, and so I didn't. I spent the night there. I slept, finally, dying the little death. . . .

And dreamed that I was buried alive. I had been searching for a soft darkness to hide myself in, always knowing that the only perfect peace was the grave . . . until at last I dug myself a pit too deep to crawl out of. At last I lay down, to let oblivion spill in on me; welcoming the darkness from which there would never be a morning.

But instead of peace I knew only horror—smothering, blinding, paralyzing horror. I cried out to Death: It was a mistake, I wasn't ready, it wasn't time, *let me go back!*

And Death appeared, wearing the face of a madwoman dressed in rags, holding morning in her hands as she asked me, "What would you give for this?"

"Anything!" I cried. But I had nothing left to give her; I had thrown it all away.

"There is no more time," she said. And Death swelled and spread and opened gaping jaws of blackness . . . a roaring, rumbling fury rose out of the depths of the earth to claim me. The earth shook, dirt cascaded onto me from the rim of the open grave—

Terror woke me, to the light of a new morning—to the ground shaking beneath me, to a rumbling that seemed to rise through the planet itself. To a white plume of water boiling in the mist, forty meters high. I stared at it, stared at the shrouded world around me in dumbfounded panic. . . . *Ang's geyser!* I scrambled to my feet and ran back toward the rover, suddenly far more afraid of being left behind than I was of facing Ang or Spadrin again.

The rover materialized like a vision out of the fog. I halted in my tracks, panting, trying to get my panic under control. Ang and Spadrin stood beside the vehicle, watching the geyser. Ang looked away abruptly, as if he sensed my presence. "Gedda!" he shouted, and gestured at me.

I joined them, not looking at Spadrin. I felt his mocking stare burn the S into my forehead.

"Where the hell have you been?" Ang said. "We've lost two days."

"Two days?" I said stupidly. I looked at my watch—my watch was gone. And suddenly I saw that my hand was clenched in a fist, realized that it had been that way since I woke. I pried my fingers open . . . saw the uncut solii that lay in my palm. My hand knotted convulsively, before anyone else could see the stone. Dimly I remembered seeing footprints in the sand around me, where there had been none before. . . . "But I was only gone overnight. I . . . slept out." I waved a hand back the way I'd come.

"Two days!" Ang was as sure of it as I was. "I searched all over. Thought you fell into a goddamn crater, or got swallowed up— I told you never to do that!"

"I don't understand. . . ." I felt my face, felt only the barest stubble of beard, and the scab of a half-healed bite on my jaw. I didn't feel hunger or thirst enough for two days. But he was as sure as I was; *and he hadn't found me.* I felt as if something was trying to strangle me. I wiped my hand across my mouth.

Ang shook his head. Maybe that was meant to be an answer. "Let's go. That geyser only lasts about an hour. I don't want to lose another day."

Spadrin climbed into the rover's cab. Ang hesitated, staring at the mark on my forehead. "Thanks," I murmured. "Thanks for waiting two days." I knew Spadrin wouldn't have waited.

He only shook his head again, and followed Spadrin up.

DAY . . .

I don't know what day it really is. Have I been out here all my life? It hardly matters. The rover is a reeking oven. My clothes are unbearable; I've given up and stripped to my shorts with the others. My skin is peeling off like tissue, like a sunburn, from the allergies.

We found the next part of Ang's trail easily enough, anyway. We've been following the dry riverbed for a couple of days, I think . . . a few days. A week. More wastes of salt and alkali. . . . In the distance now I can see plumes of smoke—volcanoes, Ang says. This is rift country, where the planet's crust is thinnest. Its molten core boils up out of cracks, to shatter the permanence of our illusions. Somewhere out there is Fire Lake. Waiting for me—

And Song, waiting too. Why? Why are you there? Sibyls *are* permanence and stability, the sanest people alive. Why would you run away into this? What knowledge were you seeking, what pain were you escaping from? Your picture can't tell me.

It's only a picture . . . and yet, sometimes I feel as if I could reach into it and touch you.

But you're all unreachable—sibyls live everywhere at once, waiting to be called into someone else's mind, to answer a stranger's need. The way you answered my need. You found me in the wilderness and you saved me. You delivered me from my enemies, you gave me the gift of my life.

So that I could throw it away again, the day I left you on Tiamat. And now I'm sinking into quicksand, and I can't help myself. . . . Thank the gods you can't see me now. At least you'll never have to know the truth about me, the way my father did.

But I still need you. I need you more than ever . . . if I could only find you, touch you, hold you, make you mine the way I should have, everything would be right again—

You gave me back the future. And now I'm lost in it; like a wretched dog howling after the moon.

ANOTHER DAY.

This one was the worst yet. We lost most of our food today—thanks to Spadrin and his selfish, craven stupidity.

He got into another argument with Ang a few days ago, about his using the rover's main power access for his plugheading. Even Ang finally agreed that the rover's electrical system shouldn't be used for anything unnecessary. He ordered Spadrin to stop.

So Spadrin found another power supply—the unit that kept the perishable food in stass—and he burned it out. But he didn't tell anyone. He didn't even know what he'd done, the cretin.

No one did, until we ate breakfast—and spent the rest of the day doubled up with cramps and nausea. Food poisoning; we were lucky it didn't kill us. When I could think again about anything besides the pain in my gut, I checked the food locker's field generator, and found the short. I told the others. Even Ang couldn't ignore the look on Spadrin's face as he realized what he'd done—not just to us, this time, but to himself.

"How long?" Ang asked.

"I don't know what you're talking about," Spadrin said. He wiped his mouth, wiped perspiration off of his face.

"You used that damn joybox again! How long ago?" Ang dragged Spadrin up from his bunk with a sudden violence that startled me.

"Th-three days," Spadrin gasped. "Just three days—"

Ang shoved him down onto the bunk again. "Then it's all ruined! You ruined our food. Why the hell didn't you say something three days ago?"

"I didn't know," Spadrin said sullenly. "How the fuck would I know?"

"You knew you'd blown something, you stupid bastard. Why didn't you tell Gedda?"

Spadrin glared at me. "He's supposed to take care of that shit himself. It's his fault."

"I can't fix something if I don't know it's out!" I pressed my hands against my stomach and sat down.

"He's right," Ang said, meaning me, for once. "It's your goddamn fault, Spadrin. If we don't have enough supplies to get us to my strike—"

I looked up at him, and in that moment I realized that he would kill Spadrin, kill us both, if he thought we stood in the way of his obsession. "Listen, Ang," I said, trying to sound calm, "we still have plenty of freeze-dried left. We have enough water. If we ration it out we shouldn't have a real problem. You said we were getting close—"

He met my eyes, but he wasn't seeing me. "You can't count on it, out here. You can't count on anything. . . ." He picked up the plate of food that he'd dropped when the sickness hit him. He balanced it on his palms like an offering.

"Well, that's life," I said softly, wondering how I would ever reach Fire Lake now. My hands clenched. "I'll find a way—" I whispered, not meaning to say it aloud.

Ang stared at me, and sanity crept slowly back into his expression. "You're right." He nodded; his mouth twisted into a grimace of irony. "We'll get there. We'll do it on half rations, we'll do it on nothing, on our hands and knees, if we have to." He looked at me again, and at Spadrin hunched miserably on the bunk. Deliberately he wiped the food off the plate onto the floor in front of Spadrin's feet, and then he twisted the thin metal plate between his heavy hands, crushing it, still looking at us. He turned and went forward into the cab, as if we were no longer there.

We're still alive; still searching, still following the dead river up-stream. We've been in these clown-striped badlands for days.

Today we finally met another pilgrim, here in this twisting maze of canyons. He was leading a huge whillp, one of those rubbery, glistening things from Big Blue that secrete acid to suck nourishment out of the rock, and never eat or drink. It was loaded down with sacks and containers, and it oozed along the canyon at barely walking speed.

I couldn't imagine how long the man must have been out here, moving at the whillp's pace. I decided it was too long, because when he saw us he wasn't afraid. He stood in the middle of the dry wash, waving his arms, shouting and grinning through his pale beard as if we were the best thing he'd ever seen.

Ang stopped the rover and we got out. Even the sight of three sweating, filthy, armed men didn't wipe the smile off of his face. Spadrin stood on one side of me; his eyes were narrow and cold. Ang stood on the other; his face was grim with a kind of tension that I'd never seen on it before. I felt my hands clutching my gun too hard—more because of their expressions than the stranger's.

"Halloo, halloo," the stranger shouted, coming toward us with outstretched, empty hands. He started to speak in a foreign language—after a minute I recognized it as Kesraal. That meant he was from Big Blue, like the beast. He stopped in front of us, just short of trying to embrace somebody. He looked at our guns and his face fell, as if we'd insulted him instead of threatened him. He jabbered earnestly, raising grizzled eyebrows.

"What's he want?" Ang muttered, rhetorically. He scratched himself.

"He asked if he's offended us somehow," I said. "His name is Harkonni, and he's from Big Blue. He's very glad to see us— we're the first people he's seen in almost a year."

Ang looked at me, surprised.

I shrugged. "I speak a few languages." I felt something stir in me that I'd almost forgotten the name of.

Spadrin snorted, and gestured with his rifle. "Then tell him to get out of our track, or we'll be the last people he ever sees."

I saw the stranger start and frown at Spadrin. "I don't think he needs it translated. You understand what we say?" I asked Harkonni in Kesraal.

He nodded, still with the hurt look on his face. "Yes, yes." He answered in the language we were all using, this time. "I understand you. Forgive me, I forgot. I have not had the tongue of this world in my mouth for a long time."

Spadrin laughed out loud at the incongruous image, and even Ang's mouth inched upward.

Harkonni grinned, obviously missing the fact that they were

laughing at him. His pale eyes were too bright, the eyes of a man with a fever. They were startlingly blue against his sun-burned face. I shifted from foot to foot uneasily.

"Yes, yes," he went on. "It is wonderful to hold conversation with you today. Wonderful to see you all. Are you prospectors like myself?" There was only one other thing we could be, but that didn't seem to worry him.

Ang nodded. He lowered his gun. Spadrin didn't.

"I would like to share some food and talk with you," Harkonni said, with a kind of pathetic eagerness.

"Food? You have a lot of food?" Spadrin asked.

Ang looked uncertain, but he nodded. "I guess we can spare an hour."

"This is wonderful!" Harkonni beamed. "I have so much to tell! I haven't seen anyone in a year! I'll even tell you my secret. I made a strike—"

"Wait!" I said in Kesraal. "Don't tell us that. It's not worth it—save your secrets until you reach civilization."

Spadrin glared at me. "What did you say to him?"

"He told me not to trust you," Harkonni said earnestly. "But it's all right, I trust you—"

Spadrin swung his rifle butt at me before I could move, and knocked me down. "Keep your mouth shut!"

"Spadrin!" Ang shouted. "For the love of the Aurant, not here!" He pulled me to my feet. "You self-righteous ass," he muttered at me. "You beg him for trouble."

I folded my arms across my aching ribs, and leaned against the rover's front end until I could breathe again.

Harkonni was half frowning, now, like a man waking up in a strange bed.

"So you made a strike?" Ang said. "Lucky man. Whereabouts—

up there?" He pointed in the direction we were heading; his hand jerked with tension.

Harkonni nodded a little uncertainly, as if he couldn't stop himself from answering even if he wanted to. "Yes, yes, all over the ground, up there, all over—"

Ang swore and pushed past him, running toward the pack beast. "They're mine, goddamn it! I found them first—"

Harkonni ran after him. "No! Leave them alone! It's my treasure—" He clawed at Ang's shoulder. Spadrin followed them and struck Harkonni with his rifle butt, knocking him down. Ang went through the bags until he found the one he was looking for. Harkonni sat protesting on the ground, with Spadrin's stun rifle pointing into his face.

Ang jerked the bag open and plunged his hand into it, pulling out a handful of lumps. He looked down at what he held, and the blind greed in his eyes turned to incredulity. "Shit!" He flung the handful away, and dumped the bag's contents onto the ground. "It's nothing but shit!"

At first I thought he only meant that he hadn't found what he wanted. But then I saw his face. I pushed away from the rover and went to where he stood looking down. Scattered on the ground around his feet were small brownish-gray lumps of dried excrement.

I looked from Ang's face to Harkonni's, and Spadrin's. "Gods!" Spadrin muttered. His mouth twisted with disgust. The stun rifle quivered in his hands. For a minute I thought he was going to fire it into Harkonni's terrified face. At that range the charge would kill him. Harkonni began to cry. Spadrin stepped back and away from him, as if killing him was beneath even Spadrin's dignity. "Let's get out of here."

Ang nodded and dropped the bag he was still holding onto

the pile of dung. He wiped his hands on his shorts. His face was empty of everything but relief. "It's still up there." He looked away, following the whillp's shining acid-etched trail on up the canyon with his eyes. "My treasure." He started back to the rover. Spadrin grabbed up a sack of Harkonni's food supplies and followed him.

"My treasure, my treasure . . ." Harkonni sobbed. He crawled past me toward the pile of dung.

"Gedda!" Ang called. "Come on!"

I went back to the rover, almost running to get away from the sound of Harkonni's weeping.

"I can feel it, I can almost smell it!" Ang said this morning. He got us moving when it was barely dawn, he was so sure we'd find his treasure today. The fault-broken terrain ahead of us was stained a rust red. He swore it would hold the solii formation. He set the rover's tracer equipment to close-scan for the proper mineral compounds. He was so sure. . . .

The sky was filled with black and purple clouds, the way it often was in the late afternoons, turning the light-washed badlands sullen and dark ahead. Lightning flickered and a few fat drops of rain pockmarked the dust on the windshield, making a promise the clouds never kept. Thunder rolled over and around us like the laughter of the gods. And we came to the end of Ang's journey.

Ang was piloting, like he usually did—today he was even humming tunelessly. He'd never done that before. Spadrin stole stale snapper biscuits from my plate while I tried to eat standing up, pressed into a corner of the cab. His eyes dared me to stop him. I didn't even care—the heat, the stink, the food poisoning, had killed my appetite days ago. Only Spadrin had any appetite left, like the animal he was.

Then suddenly the rover lurched to a stop, so abruptly that I lost my balance and knocked over Spadrin's bottle of ouvung. It spilled on his leg. He swore at me, and grabbed my wrist. "Clean it up, Gedda." He jerked me down; I saw his knife blade glint and then disappear. I pulled off the rag I was wearing as a sweatband. On my knees, I began to wipe the liquor off of his leg. But he stood up suddenly, pushing me aside. "Ang, are we there?" He was looking past Ang's shoulder.

Ang sat silently behind the controls, staring out at something. Sweat trickled down his neck. His hands lay in his lap, clenched into white-knuckled fists.

"Ang!" Spadrin shook his shoulder.

Ang reached up and opened the door. He got to his feet. Without a word, he climbed out and down. Spadrin leaped down after him. After a moment I followed them outside.

They stood on the edge of a cliff, with the wind whipping their hair. I made my way between rust-red boulders to the precipice. Below me the wall of rock dropped sheerly into a purple abyss. The far rim of the canyon was hundreds of meters away; the bottom must have been a good half a kilometer below us. Down in its shadowy depths I saw a river winding like a snake. A river of light . . . of molten lava. The crack in the earth ran as far as I could see, looking to the left. And looking right, I saw on the horizon an immense surface of blazing light, like a sun fallen to earth . . . *Fire Lake*. Elation filled me. *At last.*

"It can't be!" Ang shouted. "This can't be here, it can't!" He looked at the rover, as if it had somehow betrayed him. He looked down into the abyss again. He took a step forward, as if he were going to challenge its reality. I caught hold of his arm. He pulled loose, frowning, but he moved away from the edge.

Spadrin shouldered me aside. I backed up, away from both of them. "What's this mean, Ang? Ang?" Spadrin said. "Where's the treasure? Where are the soliis? Ang—!"

"I don't know. . . ." Ang whispered. "This shouldn't be here. We can't be *here*—" He gazed toward the shining horizon, toward Fire Lake. "You can't do this to me!" he screamed at the sky.

"You mean there's no treasure? You mean we came all this way for nothing—and now we're lost?" Spadrin jerked him around. "You fucking dirtsider, is that what you mean?" He struck Ang across the face.

Ang lunged at Spadrin, but Spadrin threw him down on his back and sat on his chest, holding his arms flat. "Is that what you mean—?"

Ang turned his face away, looking out into the canyon. "Yes," he whispered. "Yes." Tears crept out of his eyes and dripped into the dirt.

Spadrin got up off of him, and let him get to his feet. Ang stood at the edge of the abyss with his back to us. His tall, broad-shouldered body seemed to wither.

Spadrin stepped forward again and pushed him over the edge.

"No!" I shouted, but Ang's cry as he went over obliterated the sound. I ran forward—but it was far too late by the time I reached the rim. Ang had already stopped screaming. I saw his body rebounding from the rocks far down the wall. I turned away from the edge, shutting my eyes.

Spadrin still stood at the top of the cliff, watching Ang's body fall toward the planet's core. I heard his laughter before I let myself look at him again—high, strangled laughter edging toward hysteria. "Gedda," he gasped, "get the rover started."

I didn't move or answer. I felt as though I had become a part of the stone; as though I had been standing that way for millennia. . . .

He looked over at me, the crazy laughter disappearing from his face. "I told you to move." His voice was like a knife.

"Why?" I said. "You've killed Ang. You're lost. You'll never find your way back."

The hysteria still burned in his eyes. "Don't say that. Don't say it." His hands flexed.

I looked away, toward Fire Lake lying on the horizon. Its brilliance turned my vision molten. I stood waiting, waiting. . . .

Spadrin's footsteps closed in on me, his hand on my arm wrenched me around. My eyes were fire-blind. He shoved me. He shoved me for the last time.

I don't remember the blow that tore my knuckles and bloodied his face. I don't remember the blow that knocked him down. I only remember that I was strangling him, beating his head against the ground, when my rage cleared again . . . that my voice was raw from shouting curses, from shouting, "You killed him! You killed him!" over and over and over. Spadrin lay as limp and senseless as a rag toy when I let go of him at last, and his blood was the color of the stone.

I took the knife sheath from his arm and strapped it to my

own. I got the guns from the vehicle's locker and threw them all over the cliff, except for the one that I slung at my back. Then I dragged Spadrin to the rover and poured half a bottle of ouvung over his head.

He came awake, cursing and dazed; he tried to get to his feet as soon as he recognized me. But he slid down again as his body refused to obey him. The look of disbelief on his face was almost funny. "Wha—?"

I took a long drink from the open bottle, holding the gun on him. "All right, murderer," I said. "I'm taking over this vehicle now." I kicked him. "Get inside. We're leaving."

Hatred and fear warred in his eyes. "You think you can take me back?" He pulled himself slowly up the rover's side.

I shook my head, and took another drink. "We're not going back. We're going to Fire Lake."

The fear stayed on his face, but his disbelief came back. "Fire Lake? You crazy—" His hand felt surreptitiously for his knife. His bruised mouth worked, but nothing came out of it for a long moment. *"Why?"*

"I'm looking for something." I hurled the bottle away, and wiped my mouth with the back of my hand. My hand was shaking. I tasted blood.

"Then you're looking for somebody to cut your throat—and mine," Spadrin snarled. "I'm not going any deeper into this hell."

"You haven't got any choice," I said. "Unless you want to stay here with Ang." I bent my head toward the cliff edge.

Spadrin's face turned the color of ash. I watched him realize what he'd do in my place.

I nodded. "If you want to survive, you bastard, it'll be on my terms."

"Gedda," he whined, "listen, don't be a fool. We can work a deal, we can still be rich! We'll go back, there are other ways to—"

"Shut up," I said. I nudged him with the gun. "Get inside."

He obeyed.

I don't understand it. I don't understand it. We've been travel-ing toward Fire Lake for days, but it never gets any closer. It's the terrain; it must be the terrain. We have to detour and back-track, we tie our trail in knots. I don't know what I'm doing with this damned thing, or how much longer it can hold to-gether now. Ang's ghost haunts it. The stale smell of his fesh sticks hangs in the air, like an obsession. . . .

I was a fool not to leave Spadrin behind. He's like a time bomb, just waiting for the right moment. If I had his guts I'd have killed him. . . . No, no, damn it! I'm an officer of the law, not an animal.

I lock myself into the cab with the controls at night, so I can sleep. I have to watch him constantly. He pretends to servility, but I can see the hatred in his eyes.

He won't stop me. I swear to you. I swear it. Nothing will stop me, I've come too far. I know now that this was meant to be. Why else would everything have happened the way it has?

Why else do I see Fire Lake on the horizon now? My body aches for you, you torture my dreams. . . . Before, I was lost and I found you. Our time will come again, and this time it will never end.

Today it rained. It rained black mud. Things like worms smeared the windshield. Spadrin got hysterical and I had to knock him out. I made him go outside and scrape off the dome after it stopped raining.

We're still no closer.

I lost the rover today. I knew I should have gotten rid of Spadrin.

I was trying to guide us through a boulder-choked gully, when he jumped me. He tried to bash in my skull with a bottle; but I've grown almost prescient. I dodged the blow and knocked the bottle out of his hands. But I had to let go of the controls. The rover ran up onto the rocks and flipped itself over.

We were thrown clear across the cabin when it happened. The fall almost finished what Spadrin started. I came within centimeters of breaking my neck. My shoulder hurts like hell. Spadrin was luckier, all he got was a knot on his head. . . . Or maybe I'm still the lucky one: I stayed conscious. I got the rifle. Except it doesn't work. The integrator must have shattered. But he doesn't know that.

When Spadrin saw the rover lying on its back like a stranded beetle, he fell to his knees and beat his fists on the ground, screaming curses. And then, he looked up at me, with spittle dripping from his lips, and said, "You're crazy! You're fucking crazy! You don't even care!"

I only smiled, because I know what he couldn't know—that it didn't matter. Nothing mattered—not Ang, not him. They were only tools, the means to an end. Because this was meant to happen. "Pick up the supplies," I said. I waved the gun. "Let's get going."

We are getting closer. We are. We are. This is right. I feel it in my bones. I feel the heat of Fire Lake burning through my eyelids when I close my eyes. I feel it throbbing in my chest. It warms me when the stones we lie on crack and groan with the night's chill, and I watch its glowing beacon through sleepless hours of darkness. It purifies my blood, it leads me through the scorching days, through the valleys of death toward a . . . toward a . . . I'm afraid. I'm afraid.

Gods, when did I say that? Was I delirious? Was it the drugs? Maybe I shouldn't take them, all the painkillers and the stims. . . . How can I go on without them? But damn it, I can't afford to lose control again. How many days . . . Has time stopped?

I haven't slept at all. I've got to have sleep—but I can't sleep, with Spadrin waiting. A deathwatch beetle, waiting for the moment when I close my eyes. . . . That bastard, *he* can sleep, he's sleeping now, gods rot him. If only the gun worked, I could stun him. I want to strangle him where he lies. But I can't. I *need* him. I can't carry the supplies myself. My shoulder's too bad, I can't even touch it, I can't use my arm. Maybe I should dump them. I don't need food. Every time I try to eat I puke. . . . I'm getting weaker.

And he knows it. He keeps testing me, moving in on me. He wants to catch me off guard. I hardly dare to turn my back long enough to piss. One good arm is still all I need to aim the rifle . . . but I think he's beginning to suspect why I don't use it.

We are getting closer. I'm not dreaming that. How many days is it. . . . Too many. We're nearly out of water, anyway. But gods, we're almost there!

Help me, Song—I know you see me, you need me, you know I'm coming to you. I can almost reach you now, reach into this picture, feel your silken silver hair flow over my fingers like moonlight. Feel your lips on mine. Thou are as fair as aurora-glow. . . .

At last. At last . . . this is how it happened, at last.

I woke up. It was night, but the rocks beside me glowed, dim and bloody. I thought, *I'm awake.* And for a second I didn't understand the fear that filled me when I realized it. I rolled over—the ground and the sky swam with the pain in my shoulder. I sat up, reaching with my good arm for the stun rifle. It was gone.

Then I looked up, and saw where it had gone. Spadrin stood over me with the gun in his hands, grinning. He aimed it at my face and pressed the stud. Nothing happened. "That's what I thought," he said. He drove the gun butt into my bad shoulder. I screamed.

He laughed, and threw the gun away. He dragged me to my feet, pushing me up hard against the wall of the wash. I clung to the rough stone, sick with pain. His hand caught in my hair and jerked my head back, until I had to look at him. "I owe you a lot, Gedda," he whispered. He struck me, almost casually. "And now you're going to collect." He hit me again, harder, and there was blood in my mouth. "Where do you want me to start, *gedda*? Here—?" His fingers jabbed at my throat, and I retched. "Or here?" He twisted my sprained arm until I screamed again. "Or here—?" Pain exploded in my groin; I fell to my knees, sobbing helplessly. "What are you the most afraid of?" He waited for my mind to clear, until I was sane enough to understand again, and then he stepped back to study me. As he moved, a red glow lit his face. He looked toward the light, and froze. "No!" he murmured. "No, it can't be . . . !"

His sun-blistered face hung above me like a bloody moon: the face of an animal, the face of my enemy. I wanted to kill him. I wanted it more than I wanted to live— And suddenly his knife was in my hand, instead of in its hidden sheath. I looked down at it with a kind of hunger. My fist tightened around its hilt; its blade shone red. "Spadrin!" I hissed.

Disbelief swelled his eyes as he saw the knife. He backed away from me, stumbled and went down. I threw myself on top of him and pressed the knife to his throat.

"Gedda," he gasped, "don't, don't! I didn't mean it, I swear by the Unspoken Name! I'll do anything . . . name it, name it, what do you *want* from me!"

There was only one thing I wanted from him. I raised the knife, letting it hang in the air above him while I watched his face.

"*Please*—" he blubbered.

I smiled. And then I drove the knife into his chest.

He screamed, thrashing on the ground under me. I held him there, pulling the knife out of him. Blood spurted over my hands, splattering my face, as he died. The life went out of him like a sigh.

But I drove the knife into him again, and again; because it

wasn't enough, because he deserved so much more . . . because it felt good. And with every death the poisoned blood poured out of him, another demon flew up—he was filled with demons, too much monstrous evil for one human body to contain. I saw every one of his faces, I knew every one of his secret names—I killed him over and over and over. And every time I destroyed another I was freer; I would be free forever when I destroyed them all—

I killed him and killed him and killed him. . . .

The antique watch began to chime, disturbing the funereal silence of his office, in which he sat like a mourner. Gundhalinu stirred at last; time present began to flow again. He raised an unsteady hand to his belt and shut off the recorder; took the watch from his pocket, listening to its familiar music.

But still the ghosts would not leave him. . . .

I'm free! I'm free free free freefreefreefreefreefreefreefreefree. . . .

I sit laughing in the turbid sand, laughing, laughing. . . .

The deathwatch beetles begin to gather around me, clicking their mandibles in mourning. I scramble up with a curse, leaving them to their business. Looking down at Spadrin's corpse, suddenly I wonder what he saw that made him look away from me. The glowing blackness whispers secret words, and somehow I know what the answer must be—

It is. Beyond the curve of wall I see it at last, waiting. Fire Lake. I run shouting and crying out of the shadows onto the shore, the endless beach of congealed rock leading down to the shining sea. It is all black and red, death and blood. I fall to my knees in wonder. The sky is completely starless, and the molten Lake fills the darkness with fire, a singularity in the heart of night.

The gnarled stone of the beach is as warm as flesh beneath my touch. The surface has congealed into the sightless eyes and gaping mouths of a million tiny faces; they scream soundlessly beneath my weight, my probing fingers. I crawl over them toward the perimeter of the Lake.

But suddenly figures block my way. *Not alone*—*?* I sit back, cradling my throbbing arm. Looking up, I know them, these shuffling, trilling matchstick forms.

The cloud ears ring me in like a tumbledown fence. I push myself to my feet within their circle. The missionary woman we left in the steaming valley stands before me in a corona of light, her ragged arms outstretched. "Have you discovered the true nature of time?"

"You," I murmur. "How can you be here? We left you in the steaming valley days ago. . . ."

"Months and months ago." Her voice comforts me. She takes my hands gently, peering into my eyes. Her face is hidden in shadow. She begins to turn me in a shuffling dance between light and darkness.

"Months and months . . . ?" I say, stumbling over my feet.

> *Eynstyn and B'ryllas lost all track of Time,*
> *When Time went to sea in a bottle by Klyn.*

I sing the old rhyme, laughing as her face goes into darkness again. "Time is adrift on Fire Lake!" I shout exultantly. "Time is at sea!" I realize that she is not mad at all, but speaking perfect sense. "Moon, Moon, our time is coming. . . . Ah, gods—"

I see the old woman's face again, but a frown is filling it up. Her eyes are suddenly white with fear, looking down at my hands. "Where are the others?" she asks, pulling away. Her eyes are clear and sharp.

"The others?" I shrug. "They're dead. Spadrin killed Ang.

I killed Spadrin. He's lying over there. I stabbed him, and I'm glad." I look at my red-stained hands. "He deserved it."

She backs away from me. "No," she mutters, "no, no, no. You understand nothing. Don't touch me. It's too late for you—"

"There is no late!" I call, reaching after her. "There's no time like the present, no time to lose, no time at all— Wait!"

But the cloud ears close around her like a rattling forest, and she flees with them toward the wall of shadows.

I try to run after them. I stumble and fall, and the sky and the sea change places—black and red, red and black . . . blackness.

I wake, to the sun's fiery face drowning in light at the sky's blue-black zenith. Sweat burns in the cracks of my parched lips. I lift a hand to shield my eyes from the glare—but a shadow blocks out the sun, falling on me like a blow. I push myself up. I am ringed in again by figures. This time they are all human, all men, all armed. Their hard, closed faces and ragtag clothing tell me half a dozen different stories, all with the same ending.

"There's a dead one over here!" a voice calls. A grunt of disgust. "Nothing left on him worth taking."

One of the men who watch me gestures with his hand. The others pull me back down, spread-eagling me on the ground. He straddles me, looking down. He has mottled skin, a thick red-gold braid and beard. He must weigh close to a hundred and fifty kilos. "Search him." They do. They take the knife sheath from my arm. They take the pouch from my belt. "You kill him?" Goldbeard asks me.

"Yes!" I shout hoarsely.

"Why?"

"He deserved it."

Goldbeard grins. I can see in his eyes that he understands. And that he will probably kill me because he does. He steps away from me. One of the men tosses him my belt pouch. He kneels down, emptying out the contents. I struggle and curse.

He picks up the solii first, turning it in his hand. "Well, well, pilgrim." He grins again at me, flipping it into his own pouch.

"Hey!" one of the other men calls. "He was my spot! I got mineral rights on him."

Goldbeard only shrugs. "You get him when I say. He's got a strike somewhere, you can pull it out of . . ." He picks up the animal foot, looks at me again, with his face twisting. He flings the foot away. His hand falls on the holo. He picks it up. He stares. "Song!" he whispers. He touches the picture to his lips, his forehead, in a kind of ritual. And then he looks at me again with rage in his eyes. "Where you get this?"

"She isn't who you think she is," I warn him. I try to control my own outrage as his fingers violate her image.

He cocks his head, half frowning. "I know that," he murmurs.

"I've come to take her away."

"Take her away?" he roars. "Take her away?" He starts toward me. "I'll see you in hell 'fore you ever see Sanctuary, you goddamned—" He stops as a splinter of reflected light lodges in his eyes. He looks down at my pouch, at something half hidden beneath its flap. He stoops over to pick it up.

The other men have tightened their hold on me, at his signal. The pain in my shoulder makes me dizzy, their faces swim and blur. I hear angry mutterings. Soon, any moment, he will give the order and they'll tear me apart. I try to lift my head, and sweat runs into my eyes.

Goldbeard stands gazing at the thing in his hand. A chain dangles from his fingers. "Sibyl—?" he asks the air, with a kind of furious dismay. "Him? You?" He turns to me again, letting the trefoil pendant drop and hang above me.

One of the others jerks at the neck of my shirt. "He no sibyl. He got no tattoo here." A knifepoint pricks my throat, stays there. He giggles as though it is tickling him.

"Yeah, but look at this—" Someone else's fingers touch my forehead. "He's got an S here." There is no pain as they trace the wound. "Maybe that's how they do it on his world."

"You a sibyl, like her? Like Song?" Goldbeard looms over me. The trefoil twists and glitters in the air between us, reflecting life and death, life and death. . . .

"Yes," I gasp. "Yes! It's mine."

His hand makes a fist over the chain. He stands glaring down at me for an eternity. I wonder what I will do if he demands that I go into Transfer. "All right," he says at last. "Let him up."

The others let me go, some in obvious relief. I sit up slowly, panting. My hand goes on its own to my forehead, to Spadrin's mark. I feel only a numb smoothness—a scar—as if it had happened years instead of days ago.

"If this is yours, put it on." Goldbeard holds the chain out to me.

I take the pendant in my hand. My fingers close convulsively until I feel the barbs pierce my flesh. I pass the chain slowly over my head, feel it settle around my neck. The outlaws shuffle back from me as I climb to my feet. I feel their frustration, their anger, their awe. None of them will touch me now.

The reeking motley and leather of Goldbeard's massive body looms before me; behind me lies Fire Lake. I see trophies hanging from his vest—jewelry, coins, teeth with inlaid gems. In the moment of hot silence that hangs between us, I hear a familiar tinkling chime. My eyes find its source—the watch, my father's antique timepiece. In my mind I see HK tucking it into his sleeve pocket. "You fool!" I mumble. "You fool."

Goldbeard eyes me warily, his hand covering the watch.

I thrust my own hand out. "Give that to me. It belongs to me."

He flinches back as if I hold a weapon. I see the fresh blood welling on my bloodstained palm, from the places where the trefoil tore my skin. He is afraid of my blood, of contamination. I step forward, holding out my hand. "Give it to me!"

He gives me the watch. A murmur of consternation passes among his men.

My eyes burn and blur as I look at the watch; my parched throat is so tight I cannot swallow. "Where . . . where did you get this?"

"Off a couple pieces of sidda shit." He laughs.

"Did you kill them?" The words feel like paper in my mouth, dry and meaningless.

Goldbeard shrugs.

I blink and blink my eyes.

"No, we didn't," one of the others says. "They were Kharemoughis. We took them back to Sanctuary and sold them."

Goldbeard pulls at his mustache. "Yeah. What you want with them, sibyl?"

"They're my brothers."

"And they stole your watch?" His mouth quirks.

"They stole more than that." My hand makes a fist; blood drips. "Take me to Sanctuary."

"You think you got a choice?" He signals to his men, and their weapons surround me. "Maybe you infected, but you not immortal. Keep it in mind."

"What are we gonna do with him, then?" one of the outlaws asks.

"Let Song decide," Goldbeard answers. They lead me down the beach to their rover.

We rise up and up on the erratic currents of heated air. Fire Lake reaches as far as I can see. Its surface shifts and flows like the face of the sun, now in sharp detail, now soft and amorphous. I rub my eyes.

As the shore disappears into the heat-haze behind us, I see something born out of the shimmering play of light ahead. A monolith of red stone rises from the center of the Lake. As we draw near it, I see water falling from its heights, plumes of liquid transfiguring into clouds as they meet the Lake's surface far below. My parched throat aches at the sight of it. I ask someone for a drink. The outlaws ignore me. The rover circles like a carrion bird high in the air, then spirals downward toward a landing.

There are buildings below, I realize at last. They are almost invisible, because they have been gouged and piled up out of the red stone itself. And then jumbled. Jagged boulders, fissures and irregularities, are fused randomly into building walls, layered between levels of mortared stone, transforming an unnatural intrusion into an artless act of chaos. They are ruins—but like no ruins I have ever known. Cleaving their heart is a twisting cross of deep canyons. Where the canyons meet is a fountainhead. Water rises out of a hidden wellspring, flows over the rock face and falls from its precipice into fire, only to rise again—

We land easily on a flat slab of stone near the canyon's edge. There are other flyers and rovers there already—I feel surprise when I see so many. I wonder dimly how many still belong to their original owners.

I look over the canyon's edge as we leave the rover. The water far below is as clear as crystal, and in its depths I see the red rock stained with cool, mossy greens. Where the canyons cross, something silvery catches the sun. The water undulates sinuously as it flows, and at first I can't think why it looks so strange. Then I realize that the glistening water surface clings to the contours of the stone as it flows along the canyon bottom, defying gravity and all reason. The wonder and the beauty of it leave me astonished. *When I wake up, I must remember this. . . .*

Goldbeard and his men lead me through the ruined town, along a rough path that follows the canyon's rim. The heat is like something alive, riding my back. I stagger under its burden. The other quarters of the town dance and swim; they seem insubstantial as I look back at them across the chasm. I search for a familiar face, for any face— There is almost no living being anywhere. Only a few ragged, shuffling wretches pass us by, never looking up. Some wear chains. "Where is everyone?"

"You'll see," one of the outlaws answers behind me. From somewhere in the distance I hear a wail of agony or madness. He pushes me to make me walk faster.

Soon we have left the town behind, following the canyon toward the rim of the plateau. I begin to hear more voices in the distance. As we near the rim I see the gathering: human forms waver in the heated air. A bizarre platform hung with gossamer flags floats above them; at first I think it is a mirage.

But it isn't. As we join the crowd at last I see the platform still adrift, hovering impossibly in the air above the cliff. Beside us the canyon ends, and the waterfall plunges over the scarp and down. Rainbows ride on the clouds of steam that billow up below us. Fire Lake is bright like the surface of the sun.

On the silk-wreathed platform a strange pantomime is taking place. A woman stands there, cloaked in red/gold brocaded cloth that gleams in the sun. She is like a mirror reflecting fire, like a vision. Before her are three very mortal men, their hands bound behind them, roped together at the waist. They are arguing about something, denying some accusation, blaming each other. I realize finally that the shining woman is there to pass judgment on them, like a priestess, or a queen. The crowd watches, murmuring its anticipation, until the three men have finished their protests. Then, suddenly, Goldbeard shouts out, "What is the truth?"

The shining woman lifts her arms and stiffens like someone going into a trance. Her voice rises eerily, filling the sudden silence that has fallen over the crowd. She speaks incoherently; her voice changes and changes again as it tries to contain a dozen other voices. At first nothing happens to the three men waiting before her. But then suddenly the distortion of the heated air around them seems to intensify; the crowd cries out in ecstasy and terror.

Reality tears apart and re-forms around me, in a split second of gut-wrenching vertigo.

A scream is echoing in my ears. My eyes are straining to see, although I don't remember the instant when they didn't see— the instant when the three men on the platform became one and a half.

The man left alive stands motionless for a long moment, staring at the half a body still bound to his own. And then he sits down, jibbering. A stream of red spills over the platform's edge.

I watch in wonder as the possessed woman comes out of her trance and sways forward to the pennant-wreathed railing. She clings there a moment, gazing down at the outcome of her judgment. Her mouth pulls back in a smile of terrible satisfaction. Somehow, using some power I cannot imagine, she has done this thing to them.

She goes to the survivor and cuts him free with a knife. Then she straightens up again, shaking her fists in the air, and calls out in a trembling voice, "This is the truth!" The survivor half scrambles, half falls down the gossamer ladder that ties the platform to reality. He crawls away, disappearing into the crowd.

The woman stands at the rail, searching the crowd with her eyes. . . . And then suddenly she has found me. She lowers her arm until it is pointing me out. It is as if she knew that I had come, as if she has staged this performance only for my sake: to show me her power. "Bring me the captive!" she calls. I see her face clearly at last, and I gasp.

"She wants you," Goldbeard says, almost resignedly. Of course she wants me. My heart leaps inside my empty chest. Goldbeard seizes my arm and pushes me forward through the crowd to the floating rope ladder, but now I am as eager as he is to reach the platform. Somehow I climb, and he follows me. The pain in my shoulder is nothing; even the Lake, lying below the trembling, swaying rungs of the fragile ladder, is nothing to me, when I know that my heart's desire is waiting.

And she is waiting—just as I remember her, just as I left her so long ago. But now she is the queen she was meant to be. Her hair falls around her like a shroud, white/black as the fields of snow, and I am snow-blind with longing. Her face is patterned with an intricate filigree of red stains. The trefoil shines against her robes. Her eyes are like moss-agate and mist . . . when she looks at me my eyes cannot break her gaze. She stands motionless, holding me with her eyes for an endless moment. The awareness of her power, over these people, over me, leaves me shaken.

Goldbeard plants a hand in the middle of my back. I stumble forward, slipping in the blood, and fall at her feet. I touch the dusty hem of her red/gold cloak. "Moon . . ." I whisper. "I knew it would be you. I knew it." I look up at her again, and her face fills with surprise.

Goldbeard kicks the severed body off the platform behind me. "We found this garbage on the shore, Song." He comes forward and pulls me to my feet; he makes her name into the name of a goddess when he speaks. "He say he's come for you. Even had your picture." She looks at him sharply, and back at me. "He's a sibyl. You want him, or—?" There is a barb of jealousy in Goldbeard's voice. I wonder if I will have to kill him.

"You're not afraid," Moon murmurs, and reaches out to touch me, as if she cannot believe I'm real. "You're not afraid of anything." She traces the scar on my forehead. "Yes . . . oh, yes," she says to Goldbeard. "I want him desperately. You don't know how long I've waited for this moment—" Her fingers feel cool and dry against my skin. She lets them wander down my cheek and across my lips. I kiss them hungrily; she pulls away. "I knew he would come someday. The Lake showed him to me. Someone who was not afraid; who knew the answer. . . . And he comes from my mother!" She gives a shrill laugh. Goldbeard looks at her blankly.

Her restless hand falls to the trefoil hanging in the gap of my ragged shirt. "Sibyl. Then the Lake called you here?"

I shake my head. "I came for you."

She frowns unexpectedly. "Do you wear this honestly?" Her eyes are too black as they stare into mine.

I shake my head again, barely.

Her hand tightens over the trefoil until the chain bites into my neck. "You will," she whispers. Aloud, she says, "The Lake has chosen another servant! The Lake has shown me his coming. . . . I claim him for the Lake; for myself." She holds my trefoil up so that it catches the light. The crowd rumbles with amazement. She looks back at Goldbeard. "Give me the solii you took from him."

Goldbeard stiffens. Slowly, reluctantly, he takes the stone from his pouch and hands it to her.

She holds it up in the air for the crowd to see, turning it between her fingers. She presses it between her palms . . . and suddenly there is a large, sparkling gemstone in her hand instead. The crowd laughs and cheers. "Your reward." She flips the gem to Goldbeard. He catches it. I watch greed and awe commingle on his face. "My Watchman," she says almost tenderly, "you've brought me the right one at last—the one I've waited for, the one I prophesied to myself."

Goldbeard's expression turns dark and uncertain. "He wants to take you away from us!" he says. The crowd's voice echoes his suspicion ominously.

"I will never leave you," she says calmly, to him, to the watchers. "I can never leave the Lake."

"Then what you want with him?" Goldbeard's eyes are hot with anger. She stares at him. He looks down, glances at the Lake with fear on his face.

She turns back to the crowd. "This speaking is over!" She raises her hands and claps them. The red/gold cloak drops from her shoulders, to lie in a puddle of blood. It is lined with black. She wears only a thin, white shift beneath it; the shift clings to her sweating body, concealing nothing. I suck in a breath of furnace-hot air. The crowd mutters and shouts its disappointment. They call out for something more, they want her to show them proof of what I am . . . they want more miracles, or more blood. But she ignores them. She ignores me, too, as if my gaze does not burn her flesh where it touches her.

"I will return to the tower," she tells Goldbeard. "Bring him."

She goes down the ladder as lightly as a ghost. Figures materialize, bearing a canopy to shade her as she walks.

I want to go after her. Goldbeard knows it; he holds his gun on me. He holds me back until she grows small in the distance, following the canyon's edge . . . until I am ready to throw myself over the rail to keep from losing her. "Nobody goes with her," he says. "You only go *to* her." He lets me leave the platform at last as she disappears from sight; his men are still waiting below. They watch me even more darkly as they take me back to town.

We cross endless plazas piled with rubble, climb shallow steps chipped into the rock face and hot shining ladders. I climb awkwardly, using one hand. There are towers rising above the maze of tumbled structures; round ones, square ones, two or three stories high, with tiny windows that stare like skeleton eyes. This place is old, older than memory. We come to a tower whose middle story is now a slab of red stone. The path to its base shines with beaten metal. A fence of bones beckons us, a human skull leers above two human guards lounging against the wall at the foot of the steps that circle it. I feel as if I know this place; that it can only belong to her, only be what I've been moving toward, all this time. . . . "Our time has come," I whisper. Goldbeard glances back at me.

We stand beneath the skull's empty gaze as the guards come forward to challenge us. They wear a grotesque parody of armor; one of them is a huge woman nearly two meters tall. The other has a pot jammed onto his head. I laugh, and they glare at me with death in their eyes. Goldbeard mutters to them in a language I don't know, and they back away from me suddenly. They let me pass, and Goldbeard with me. We leave his men behind again.

Oh gods, oh gods, this is the way of return. It is all I can do to keep from running as we climb the stairs. *Soon. Soon.* Every second is an eternity passing, every step closes the gap of time. We circle the tower of stone, pass through a heavy metal door into the chamber at its top. A breath of cool air greets us. I run my hands self-consciously over my filthy clothing: I am to appear before a queen. It is cold in the chamber, as cold as the frozen wastelands of Tiamat, and I begin to shiver.

Moon rises from a massive carven seat filled with rich rugs and pillows: a queen's throne. She holds out her hands. I start toward her, but Goldbeard jerks me back.

"Let him go!" she orders. "He is the Lake's chosen. You are not to harm him." Goldbeard lets me go, angrily. "Leave us," she says. As Goldbeard goes to the door with heavy reluctance, she calls, "We are not to be disturbed!"

We are alone. I am trembling now from the urge to take her, to feel her body—I lift my hands, drop them again.

She glances at me, licking her lips, as if she knows exactly what I want. She touches my trefoil. "The fishhooks—the bait." Her fingers slip downward to my belt and toy with the catch. "No one ever touches me. It's been so long. . . ."

I feel my erection pressing painfully against my pants. My hands make fists. *No! I'm not an animal—!* some dying thing inside me cries.

She smiles at me—a strange, guarded smile, not one that I have ever seen on her face before. "Why did you come? Why is it you, after so many . . . ?" Her eyes seem all pupil, all-knowing.

"I had to," I murmur. "You know I had to."

"Yes." She nods. "I know. Tell me who you are."

"BZ," I say desperately, searching her face for a sign. "BZ, Moon, Police Inspector BZ Gundhalinu! Have I changed so much?"

She looks my ragged, bloodstained body up and down with gentle amusement. "Tell me who I am?"

"Moon! Moon, for gods' sakes, don't— You found me in the wilderness, you saved me. You gave me back my life . . . you made me forget my scars." I hold out my wrists to her. "And then I left you to him! To that polluted weakling you thought you loved. I thought it was right; I thought I had to obey the code, and do what was honorable. Fuck honor! I'm free . . . nothing means anything anymore; nothing but what I want! Nothing will come between us this time, not even time. This time I'll have you forever—" I pull her into my arms, covering her mouth with my own.

She struggles in surprise, pushing me away. Her eyes are alive with an emotion that at first I mistake for rage. She turns away from me with a curse, clenching her hands, shaking her head. Her shining hair absorbs all light. I take a deep breath and then another, trying to force my body to obey me.

Her shoulders loosen; she breathes calmly and easily again. She opens her hand as she turns back to me. The uncut solii is lying in it. I blink and smile. She closes her hand, opens it. The stone is perfectly cut and polished. It glows with secret fire. "They say it has powers of enlightenment," she says. "Swallow it, false sibyl. Make it a part of you."

I cannot refuse her. I raise it to my lips hesitantly, put it into my mouth. I feel saliva gather on my parched tongue; the stone is smooth and pleasant, and it slides down my throat like water.

She nods. "Do you see me differently now? Do you know the truth yet?"

I shake my head.

"You will."

She seizes my arm and leads me wordlessly into another room, to a bed piled with fragrant perfumed pillows. I fall across it; my legs are too weak to hold me up any longer. The room is a storehouse of strange and wonderful things heaped all around the walls; I gaze around me until my eyes blur, trying to separate one bit of color from another.

On a table by the bedside is a solitary globe filled with restless, molten light. I reach out to it, hypnotized; but just as I begin to feel its heat she brings a flagon of flowery brandy and presses it to my lips. I drink it all.

She sits beside me, watching me, waiting. "Who am I now?"

I shake my head. "Moon."

"Where did you get the trefoil?"

I turn it over in my hands. I try to remember. "It was given to me. . . ."

"A woman gave it to you. A sibyl. My mother. I know everything she does." She looks away toward the narrow window slit.

The sky is blindingly blue beyond the walls, bright/dark, like her hair. "Did she tell you I'm crazy?"

I remember. I nod.

"That's what she thinks. I see through her eyes and she sees through mine. And I hear the secrets of the universe. The Lake tells me everything. . . ." Moon's eyes glaze as if she is hearing them now. "Did she tell you why I'm this way?"

I shake my head.

"It's her fault. I wanted to be a sibyl, like her. I went to the choosing place. . . . I was judged, and refused!" She pulls painfully at her hair. "But my mother infected me anyway—" She is seeing me again; her eyes are on fire with hatred. "And now she wants me to stop tormenting her. 'Death to kill a sibyl, death to love a sibyl, death to be a sibyl!'" She beats on me with her fists. "She sent you to me, you come from her!" Her nails rake my cheek. "But I'll make you the Lake's. I'll show her—"

I catch her wrists in my hands, force her back and down across the bed. I fall on top of her, ignoring the pain, blind to everything but her face as I cover it with kisses. She fights me wildly as I hold her prisoner, pressing my body down on hers. "Don't!" I gasp. "Don't, you're Moon, I love you—"

She has opened her mouth to bite me, to infect me— She takes a deep, sobbing breath instead, staring back into my eyes. And then her eyes fill with tears. "I love you!" she shrieks, as if she hates me. "I hate you—" she cries, as if she loves me. "I love you. . . ." And she is not seeing me at all, as her eyes close and her mouth finds mine hungrily.

I rip at her clothes and my own until there is nothing against our flesh but each other's flesh. Her whole body is dyed with intricate designs. Her hands still punish me, flailing, raking my back; fury and desire are joined inside her the way I want to feel her body joined with mine. Her soft, open lips burn my cracked and broken ones with hot kisses; her tongue enters my mouth. And when her hand finds the throbbing life below my belly she seizes it with fierce urgency.

I moan. My hand fondles her breast, while the other lies buried between her legs, parting them as I probe the liquid depths of her secret places. Her body bucks and heaves, urging, demanding, as if there is no time . . . but I know there is all the time in the world now. Our time has come; everything will be right again for us—

We roll, struggling, tangling, absorbing and exploring each other until there are no secrets left. Her mouth travels down my body, licking away sweat and grime, devouring me, as she forces my face away from hers —down, down, until it is buried in her moist warmth and I taste the bittersweetness of her. Her body rises like a wave, cresting, breaking, and ecstasy bursts out of her like a scream of pain . . . another . . . and another.

And then, gasping, she seizes my manhood. Her nails are buried tormentingly in my flesh as she pulls me over on top of her. I feel my aching hardness slide into the wet folds; I thrust fiercely, burying myself deep inside her. She wraps her legs around me and I plunge ever deeper into her darkness. I thrust harder and faster, driven by the need to obliterate all memory.

And in my mind a frantic voice is crying that this is nothing like the last time, she is nothing like the last time— But it is lost, lost in the fire. I feel the life-force building inside me, feel the burning well up in my loins until there is nothing left of me except my need—

I release with a shuddering cry, and as I do she pulls me down on top of her, crushing my lips against her own. "Save me, save me—" she whimpers. My tongue enters her waiting mouth.

Her teeth close on my tongue, tearing it, and her saliva mingles with my blood.

"No—" My cry of pleasure becomes a cry of fear. I try to break free in the sudden excruciating moment when I realize what she has done. Fire in my blood, icicles in my bones, it is too late— I feel myself falling, still falling and falling, through rapture into oblivion.

The voices wake me, a thousand voices murmuring, shouting, whispering to me. I open my eyes; my body is rigid with terror. I am in a room, a strange red-walled room, sprawled on a bed, naked and alone. My body is covered with whorls and stripes of reddish-brown stain. I sit up in a spasm, shaking my head, but the voices remain, jabbering and calling. I hunch over, hiding my nakedness, even though I cannot see who mocks me. I am sick with hunger. My body aches and smarts, my tongue is sore and swollen in my mouth. I whimper, covering my ears with my hands, but the voices are inside my head. "Leave me alone!"

Someone enters the room—a woman, but it is hard to see her through the voices. I feel my own face under my hands, reach out to her like a blind man. I do not feel her touch my hand, she does not touch my hand. But I know her face. *I know her face*—*!* I shout the voices down until I can name it. I've seen it a hundred times, but only in a picture. *Song. This is Song.* And last night I saw her and did not see her as our bodies joined.

Like a dream—last night . . . last night . . . The voices are drowning me; I choke and gasp.

Song's face moves close to mine. I read her lips, her voice is lost among a thousand voices: "False sibyl, now you are a real one. Now you know what I know. And now my mother knows what she did to me!" She laughs, holding the trefoil that I wear up in front of my eyes.

I try to make words with my swollen tongue, but all I do is groan. *Gods, oh gods . . . infected . . . I'm insane!* I push her away and get to my feet, staggering across the room to the window. I look out over the town and see Fire Lake stretching to the horizon beneath the glaring blue sky. The thousand voices in my head roar even louder at the sight of it. I fall to my knees, banging my head against the stone sill.

Song is behind me, pulling me up again, shouting into my face. "You hear it? You hear the voice of the Lake! It wanted you. Now it can eat *your* mind. It will eat you alive, unless you're stronger than it is." She pushes me to the window. "You belong to Fire Lake now. Look at your kingdom."

I look out over the Lake, and its burning brilliance sucks my mind out of my body like a wail. The air shimmers above its coruscating surface. The air is alive, it flows through itself in waves. It floods with colors—now crimson, now sapphire, as the colors fold into nothingness or flower into sight. It is like a window on another world: Mirages move in the heart of the color, phantoms of that other world. The voices rise and fall inside me as the colors bloom and fade. They might even fit a pattern . . . they might almost make sense—

I bring my fists down hard on the windowsill; for a moment the pain in my hands frees my mind. And beneath the clamor of voices I feel something else coiled around my thoughts, as formless as the mumbling of the planet's soul. . . . Madness. Everything I see is a lie, infected by madness. It flashes back and back in the broken mirrors of my mind, until the weight of my own despair crushes me to the floor. My empty stomach heaves, and I sit gagging.

But when I cannot see the flaming mutation of the Lake, I begin to feel better. After a little I crawl away from the window, pulling free of Song's clutching, taunting hands, and take a blanket from the bed to cover my nakedness. I fold myself inside it and go out of the tower, down the steps. The guards let me pass; I can barely see them.

I run aimlessly through the still-shadowed levels of the broken town. The tortured buildings seem to shift and fall and reshape themselves before my eyes. There are people everywhere now, before the midday heat. I smell food cooking, and my stomach aches to be fed. I enter an open doorway and take the food that I find there, cramming it into my mouth. A shriveled old woman shouts soundlessly at me. I watch her come after me with a cleaver, but I cannot keep my mind on her. I take another piece of bread. She stops suddenly. She drives the cleaver into a tabletop, and goes out of the room.

When I am full, I go out again into the windswept square. It is swarming with figures, hundreds, thousands. Some of them wear stinking rags, some of them shine like silver. Some of them stare at me. Some of them walk right through each other. I stumble and fall, cursing with fear, the first time one walks through me. But then I realize that they must be ghosts, haunting this dead city, haunting me. . . . As I watch I begin to see that the ghosts wear auras of shadowy red and blue so that I can recognize them. Their voices travel through me with their restless spirits, some speaking in strange tongues, and some in languages that I know. The voices in my head are ghost voices. No one else hears ghosts, or sees them . . . *except Song. Song is crazy too.* I am comforted a little. I have found a clue. I realize that I am searching for something. I remember: *I am a police inspector. I search for clues.* And for a moment some insane part of me takes such pleasure in the bright coherence of the memory that I gasp with ecstasy. I stand rigid until the feeling fades.

A group of laughing men with cruel empty faces comes toward me. They circle me, gesturing, pawing me, mouthing obscenities. One of them jerks my blanket off. The trefoil catches the sunlight, flashing against my chest. They drop the blanket and hurry away. I wrap it around me again.

I wander on, past a man having a fit. He thrashes on the ground, bleeding, begging some god or other to help him. I shudder and pull the blanket over my head. I begin to run again, like the beasts of World's End that run mindlessly over cliffs.

But when I reach the brink where a canyon lies like a rip in the reality of the plateau, I stop. Red dust and pebbles swirl around my feet. Far down below me I see something silver winking in the sun. The sudden sight of it excites my helpless mind like the sight of a beautiful woman. I have no idea why. Desolation settles over me again.

The rim of the canyon is sheer. The drop is almost straight down for the first fifty meters or so. I know I am insane; I am not fit to live. I know I don't want to live like this. . . . I shuffle closer to the edge. Somewhere in my head someone is trying frantically to make me afraid. I stand at the brink, looking down, swaying.

Wait! he screams, *wait!* I close my eyes, waiting. . . . And suddenly I see Moon. I see her face in perfect memory: her face, which made me want to live. Not Song's face, nothing like

Song; how could I ever have seen one in the other? Disbelief and confusion fill me, *I must have been mad*—

I am mad . . . with sibyl madness! "Oh, Moon," I whisper, shaking my head. "I was never worthy of you." I move closer to the edge again.

"Stop it, stop it!" Moon's voice cries.

"I can't," I say helplessly. But now in my mind I am gazing out through diamond windowpanes, and below me the streets of Carbuncle at Festival time are swarming with revelers. Outside, the people of Tiamat celebrate the coming schism of our worlds; but here in the quiet sanctuary of our room, Moon and I are the two loneliest people in the universe. . . .

Her arms close around me, pulling me back, holding me. "You're the finest, gentlest, kindest man I ever knew. I won't let you—"

And at last I turn to face her; at last I take her into my arms. It seems I have loved her all my life, knowing always that she could never be mine . . . and yet this is the time of the Change, when impossible things happen. Moon—whose life is pledged to another, whose life is complete without me, whose destiny has become entangled with my own only because my own life has lost all meaning—lays aside her life to enter mine for one timeless night.

Her lips answer the question I have never dared to ask, with a kiss as warm and alive as spring. I feel her body melt against mine . . . and all my sweetest fantasies were only a pale shadow of the hours that we spend in each other's arms. My heart speaks all the words that my mind has never known how to say as I give myself to her at last. And in the moment when we lose control she cries out the words she has no right to say: "I love you, I love you. . . ."

I open my eyes at last, feeling more alive, more grateful to be alive, than I have ever been—

And suddenly I am standing on the brink of a cliff, somewhere on another world. Alone. Moon is gone, forever. I sit down at the canyon's rim, letting my feet dangle over the edge. I'm lost, because I've lost her. My life glanced off of hers like an insect beating against a light, fluttering away again with scorched wings. And now I've come to this. There is no hope here; this is the end of the world.

Yet, somehow even her memory makes me stronger: calmer, comforted. The sun warms my aching shoulder. The sinuous water far below is the most beautiful thing I have ever seen. But now I no longer want to join it.

You're still alive! my mind tells me fiercely. *Think! See.* I look over the edge again. *Question.* What I see below me is a physical impossibility, but it exists. *How? Why?*

Ghosts are impossible, I answer wearily. I see them because I'm crazy. The choir gibbers inside me.

But I saw the water before.

I think about it. *What if it's all real . . . ?* I watch the red dust sift between my fingers. *Everything I see, everything I hear? She said I hear Fire Lake. No one knows what it is. It does strange things. Maybe I'm not crazy. Maybe I'm the only one who really sees, and hears. . . .*

Hope flutters frantically inside me. I look down at the trefoil. Hope has broken wings. . . . I am insane.

I am not insane. I am not—!

"Who are you!" I shout thickly. My words echo across the canyon and inside my head. The choirs of chaos echo echo echo.

BZ Gundhalinu. Police inspector. Technician of the second rank.

I am not a lunatic. There is a pattern to all of this, if I can only find it—

"Fuck you!" I shout into the air. "What do you know? You're infected!" I scramble to my feet and run back through town, and the ghosts howl inside me.

Somehow it is almost dark by the time I reach Song's tower again. The guards try to block my way. But when they see my eyes, they let me pass.

Song is sitting in her carven throne, crooning softly. The sound sobs in the air like a lost child. Her eyes are vacant, but as she looks up at me they fill with black betrayal. I see figures moving about her in the darkening room, and at first I think they are her servants. But then I realize that they are only ghosts. She is alone, completely alone . . . except for me. "Where were you?" she cries. I avert my eyes. I go on into the next room and collapse on her bed, huddle shivering under my blanket. The coolness of the tower amazes me after the heat outside. But Song is a sorceress; she bewitched me, she is a magician. . . .

There is a portable cooling unit under the table. I open my eyes and stare at it. Slowly I begin to realize where I am, and that I am alive, still alive. I could have died today . . . but death was the easy choice.

With a kind of amazement I realize that I still want to live. *I want to live.* I think of Moon again, and suddenly life catches fire inside me. Its heat gathers in my loins and surges into my brain. I lift my head. Two shadowy figures are making love on the bed beside me. Their passion pours into my mind.

I roll off the bed with a groan. On my knees on the floor I watch myself with Song in a haze of red—our lust made visible. My body throbs with pleasure as my own ghost fills my head with inarticulate cries. I stumble back into the next room, and Song looks up at me now with hunger in her eyes, as if she shares my hallucination. *How can we share each other's madness?* But I am only listening to my blood. I drag Song from the chair onto the floor, pulling her reality into my fantasy as I surrender to my lust for her.

But she's not Moon—! my eyes shout at me. I break away from Song's lips, panting, shaking my head. *Not Moon.* Not the woman whose every touch was as warm and sweet as spring, whose gentle understanding made the joining of our bodies into something as beautiful as life itself—a celebration, a consecration . . . an act of love. *Not Moon. Not Moon. Not.*

The fire inside me turns to ashes. Loss and bitter disappointment crystallize my thoughts. I look down into the face of a stranger, seeing her clearly at last, seeing that the real need inside me is not yesterday's mindless lust, but the need to change fate, to turn back time. "No," I whisper. "I don't love you. I don't even know you. This isn't right."

Fury and frustration blaze in her eyes as she sees that I no longer want her. She shoves me off of her. "Get away from me! You're useless! You're not anything I need, you're not even a fuck!" She spits at me. "I thought you were the one who knew the answer—that's why I took you, that's why I infected you. The Lake promised him to me. But it lied. It always lies, it's like you are! You're weak, you're nothing now! Why didn't you kill yourself out there? I hate you, you failure, you lunatic—"

I see my reflection in her eyes. I don't answer her; there is nothing I can say.

A smile of horrible spite fills her face, and suddenly I remember what she did to the men on the platform. I pull away from her, terrified that she will call up her power and tear me apart. "You're afraid of me now—" she whispers. But instead she draws me closer to her, and asks me quietly, "What are the first one thousand prime numbers?"

"I don't know," I mumble. I feel a tingling, a rushing, as an irresistible force roars into my mind and swallows my consciousness whole.

I lie at the heart of a smothering unlife, in a darkness that is the denial of all being, and yet *is* . . . as ancient as stone, as infinite as space, as intimate as a second. An eternity passes inside of an instant, I grow old and die a thousand times, unmourned. . . .

Until, after an eternity, I am reborn into my own body again, whimpering mindlessly. Song sits in her chair, watching me. "What are the one hundred major exports of Kharemough?" she asks.

I don't know. And I am swept away again . . . this time to my homeworld, and with my own eyes I see the interior of the New Hall of the Republic. The famous Ramosthenit frescoes, which my mother unearthed in the ruins of Old Dimmarh, are so close to me that I could touch them. But I am trapped in someone else's body, and I am paralyzed. I can only stare and stare in helpless longing as concerned hands, the hands of my people, reach out to me. . . .

I am back with Song. Before I can even speak she asks me another question, and I am wrenched down into utter blackness again.

The game goes on and on, as her words suck me out of myself and abandon me on other worlds, or alone in the Nothing Place . . . until at last she tires of the sport, and when I come to once more she rises from her seat and stands over my strength-less body. "You see, Mother?" she screams at no one. "You see, you see—?" Weeping furiously, she runs from the room.

I lie clawing at the dusty rug, too exhausted to move. Sleep covers me with its gentle blanket.

I wake to the choir of madness. I lie where I lay last night, curled fetally on the floor. *Gods, gods. . . .* I pray, but I know there will be no answer. *Religion is only our futile attempt to force order on chaos.* My mother told me that when I was a child. Now, at last, I understand.

Mother . . . Mama. . . . But I know there will be no answer. I bury my face in my hands, drawing my knees up tighter.

"BZ . . ."

I open my eyes. I see my mother's sad, impatient face bending above me, hazed in red. She kisses my forehead and I am a child of five again. "I'm sorry," she whispers, "I have to leave you now . . . I have to go away."

I push myself up on my arms, frightened and confused, reaching out for her. "Why?" Asking the question that I have asked myself again and again through a lifetime. *What did I do wrong?*

She shakes her head, looking away from me. "Because I can't live a lie instead of a life anymore. Try to understand. . . . Be a good boy." She kisses me again, pulling away from my hands. "Good-bye." And then she leaves my room, and our home, forever.

"Good-bye, Mother. . . ." I whisper. And at last I understand.

I sit up slowly, feeling as though I have aged a hundred years. I look at my hands, expecting them to be withered and bent. But they are my own, the backs smooth and brown, scattered with pale freckles and stained with paint. My wrists are still scarred. I sigh, rubbing my aching shoulder. The pain in the abused joint is like hot needles, but I savor it. Yesterday when I woke I could barely feel it . . . yesterday when I woke I could barely see or hear. *Getting used to it,* I think, hopefully. But then I remember last night, the fresh wound that Song opened in my sanity. *The Transfer . . . the sibyl Transfer. Not some evil magic.* I try to make myself believe it was only that. I know that sibyls are human computer ports, linked to a hidden data bank—*the blackness, the heart of a machine*—and to sibyls on other worlds. *Predictable responses,* my mind insists. *Not insanity.* But real sibyls control the Transfer, they aren't lost every time someone asks a question!

Song enters the room. My hands fly up to cover my ears, and I listen with all my strength to the cacophony inside my head. Song's lips mock me as she drifts past, her sky-blue translucent outer robe trailing her like a cloud of lost souls. There is food on a silver tray by the door. She takes only a single piece of dried fruit and disappears down the steps.

I get up when she is gone. I watch from the tower window as she wanders away across the plaza, shaded beneath her canopy, trailed by guards. The people she passes bow and prostrate themselves to her; some offer her things that glitter in the sunlight. Someone gets too close to her, and suddenly Goldbeard is there, hurling him away. In the distance Fire Lake mutates restlessly and murmurs with ghosts. The moment I look at it I am possessed, lost for what seems like hours. . . .

Finally I stagger away from the window, faint with hunger and exhaustion. I force myself to choke down what is left of Song's food, although the pointlessness of eating knots my stomach. And then I go to her bed and fall across it, and sleep some more.

When I wake she is still gone. I have no idea what time it is. I wander in a daze through the empty, silent rooms of the tower. It surprises me that I am alone, that Song does not have servants surrounding her here like she does outside, to wait on her every need. *Are they all so afraid of her? Or doesn't she want her subjects that close to her?* One of the rooms is a bathroom, and it actually functions. I use it, unspeakably grateful for privacy and comfort. Water actually flows from the cracked spout of the ornate tub. I splash myself, trying to clean the grime and painted patterns from my body; too tired to wonder how I came to be painted, or to care that all I do is make more tracks in the filth. I can't remember why it matters, anyway. Shivering, I go back into the bedchamber. My clothes are still there, torn and stinking rags. I pull my pants on awkwardly; my clumsy body seems to belong to someone else. Only its pain belongs to me. I sigh as I fasten the pants, hating the touch of the stiff, dirty cloth against my raw skin, and yet somehow comforted by it. There are other clothes, better ones, among the heaps of offerings piled up around the room.

There's one of everything ever made here, I think, and hear my own idiot laughter. Jewels, tools, odd pieces of furniture and broken equipment. I pick up a leather vest woven with gems and metal and put it on like protective armor. But I see the Lake as

I glance up, and it calls me. I go back to the window again. I stand watching helplessly, gaping into otherwhere, while the Lake turns my mind inside out.

Until suddenly a familiar tinkling chime unlocks the prison of my obsession. I turn distractedly, and see my belt lying across the bed. The silvery music stops abruptly, before its pattern is complete. I rush to the bed, fumbling open my pouch. All that is left inside it is my father's watch. I shake the watch with trembling hands, and listen as it finishes its chime. I kiss it.

Time lives! Gravity still holds me to the planet's surface. Somewhere in the universe electrons spin along in orderly sub-atomic paths, planets circle suns, galaxies spiral through the night. Pattern balances chaos. The knowledge fills me with triumph . . . triumph overwhelms me, reflecting back and back in the mirrors of my insanity, until my thoughts fall to pieces.

I hold the watch up to my eyes, trying desperately to remember . . . "My brothers! I came here to find my brothers!" I shut my eyes, make myself see their faces; I rebuild my sense of purpose bit by bit out of broken fragments. . . .

And when I open my eyes again they stand before me, ragged, hazed in blue. I can see the sky through their backs. "HK? SB? Where—where are you?" I ask, barely believing what I see. "Are you alive? Tell me where—"

"You can't be serious," SB sneers. "You're going to *give* it away?"

He is not answering what I say, but the voice of some angry ghost inside my head. *Shut up!* I think furiously, trying to shout down my madness—realizing suddenly that the ghost voice I hear is my own.

But when I focus my eyes again I am alone, listening to the

memory of a conversation with my brothers . . . not the one I just had, but another one, that I know has never happened.

I get up from the bed, cursing in frustration, with the watch clutched in my hand. The room is an obstacle course of things Song has extorted from her worshippers. I kick my way through silver dishes and dismantled terminals; walking in circles, forcing myself to pass the window again and again without looking out. And every time I do, the compulsion, the yearning, the *need*, to look out at Fire Lake leaves me weak. Somehow I am the Lake's victim, as much as I am Song's. *You belong to the Lake now.* Everything she told me after she infected me must be true. I begin to believe the incredible evidence of my senses, even though I don't know how or why Fire Lake has invaded my mind. I may be crazy, but the Lake's power over me is real enough.

And if it is real, then somehow there has to be a way to break it. I go back to the bed and lie down again. I count, I calculate, I recite a dozen different alphabets out loud to keep my thoughts my own. The watch chimes, marking meaningless segments of time. Outside the window the sky darkens; the chamber fills with the glow of Song's fire globe. I begin to lose my voice, I begin to repeat myself. I try to picture Moon, the one person whose face I can still bear to see. I talk to her memory about the memories we share, trying to speak coherently . . . until gradually her memory becomes so real to me that I *do* see her, reaching out to me, in a halo of blue light. I sit up, calling her name—

I wrench myself back miserably to the multiplication tables. I count on my fingers, as my diseased mind fights me like an addict's, wanting only to surrender to chaos, to flow out into the Lake's haunted dreamworld. Struggle is pointless, chaos whispers in my head. Pattern is an illusion, order is a lie, the universe is random. Suns die, worlds collide, life is an accident, meaningless and futile. You are insane. You control nothing. . . .

"The periodic table of elements is not a lie!" I shout hoarsely, and refuse to listen. And as time crawls by I feel my confidence returning, a little. *I can hold on. It can't force me to do anything I don't want to do. I'll learn to live with it, if I have to. Song does.* But I know that I can only retain this much control by putting all my concentration into it. I can't do that forever. It's only a matter of time. . . . Despair fills me again.

And what about the rest? it cries. I'm infected! Every time I hear a question I can't answer, my mind goes out of my body. I can't live a sane life that way!

I can learn to control it.

Only a sibyl can do that. I'm not a sibyl, I wasn't chosen, I'm not right for it! I'm not strong enough. (My legs tangle in bedding and I fall.) I can't!

How do I know? I've never tried.

"But I'm *crazy*—" I sit back on the floor, striking my knees with my fists.

Not as crazy as when I came here.

I watch, stupefied, as memories that could not possibly be mine flood my mind's eye. I remember my journey here; I remember its end. . . . I saw the face of one woman on the body of another, and used her, like an animal. . . .

I murdered a man in cold blood.

"No! No, no . . ." I hold my head, knowing that the memory of the bloody knife driving into his chest will explode out of my skull, that my heart will stop, that surely now damnation will swallow me up at last—

He killed Ang! He would have killed me! I had, I had to kill him—

But not like that. Not like that. The voices in my head wail a dirge—the voices of a thousand ancestors crying my shame, avenging furies that will torment me forever for my crime. I sink down again, embracing my punishment, and my guilt. I belong here after all. This is fitting.

And yet, some small, stubborn part of my mind insists that even my guilt proves I am no longer what I was. That I am someone new, reborn. . . .

After a long time I am calm enough to remember where I am again. I hear someone enter the outer room. From the light tread, I guess that it is Song. I stumble to my feet, sick with anticipation. How can I protect my mind from her—how can I control the Transfer?

Control the Transfer. I see half the answer, in a sudden flash of clear thought . . . and maybe more.

Song appears in the doorway, her face burnished by the chamber's ruddy light. Before she can open her mouth I shout, "Question, sibyl! I have a question for the sibyl Moon Dawntreader Summer of Tiamat—" Not knowing if I ask the impossible, not caring.

"No!" Song flings up her hands in protest. But her body goes rigid and her eyes glaze as the Transfer carries her away.

I move close to her, watching her pitilessly, straining for a sign of someone else's presence. Her eyelids flutter; her eyes look at me, through me, all around me—back into my own. She gasps.

"Moon?" I murmur. "Moon, is it really you?" I brush Song's cheek uncertainly. I can't believe that I have really called her here to me.

Song's body quivers, as if someone else longs to move it.

"Yes . . ." she whispers. "BZ! How . . . what do you . . . want of me? Please . . . give me more information."

It is all she can do, imprisoned in the Transfer's eye. I try to focus my own addled thoughts, afraid that I will lose her— "I'm . . . I'm here on Number Four, at a place called Fire Lake. I need help. Something gets into my head all the time, and . . ." *Rambling! Stop it!* "I'm a sibyl, Moon! Someone infected me, the woman who sees me now for you. She wasn't meant to be a sibyl . . . she's out of her mind." I swallow painfully. "And I think . . . I think I am too. I'm trapped here, I can't get help from anyone else. Tell me how you control the Transfer! Every time I hear a question—"

"A sibyl . . ." Song's voice reaches out to me, but it is Moon who fills the words with compassion. "Don't be afraid of the infection, BZ. It doesn't have to make you insane. Fear of it can be your worst enemy. I know you . . . I know that"—Song's hands twitch—"that the finest, gentlest, kindest man I ever met must have been meant for this. That you must have been chosen, somehow. . . ." Song takes a deep breath. "It's difficult for everyone, at first. Complete understanding . . . complete control of the process takes many months. But I can give you enough to help you. There are word formulas for the channeling of stimuli, patterns that become a part of your thought processes in time, like—" she breaks off, as the sibyl mind searches for a meaningful analogy, "the adhani discipline practiced on Kharemough."

"Really? I practice that—"

"Use it, then. It will help you concentrate. But there are key words you need to make a part of it. You know that there is a kind of ritual to the formal sibyl Transfer; it starts with the word *input.* No other questions need to be recognized. Learn to block casual questions by concentrating on the word *stop*."

"*Stop?*" I say, incredulous. "That's all?"

"Yes. It's very simple; it has to be. But there's much more . . ." Her own words flow easily now, a clear stream.

I gaze into her eyes as I repeat every phrase, seeing Song's face but knowing Moon's heart and mind lie behind it. The knowledge helps me focus on her words; I am afraid to lose even one in the clamoring wilderness Song has made of my mind.

At last she has told me all that she can. ". . . it takes time. Believe in yourself. This is not a tragedy; it could be a blessing. Perhaps it was meant to be."

Never, I think, knowing the truth about what I have become. But I whisper, "Thank you." I touch Song's face again. Her eyes shine with tears. "You don't know what this means to me—" I take her hands in mine and kiss them. "I love you, Moon. I'll never love anyone else. I've hated myself ever since I left Tiamat." I take a deep breath. "I can tell you that now, because I know I'll never see you again." I try to see her as she must be— no longer a pale, stubborn barbarian girl, but a woman, a queen, the leader of her people. The once painful knowledge only makes me love her more.

Song blinks her eyes, and sudden tears run down her cheeks. "I need you," she cries, like the crying of seabirds. Her eyes begin to stare.

"Moon!" I clutch Song's shoulders, clutching at the spirit that inhabits her. My kiss smothers the last words that come to her lips: *"No further analysis!"*

Song sways; I catch her as she falls and lay her down on the bed. I straighten up again, still feeling the moist pressure of her lips against mine. *I need you.* Were those words really Moon's, or her own? She stares darkly at me, wiping her eyes, but she says nothing. I look away. Twice now I have used her body to answer my need for Moon. . . . I tell myself angrily that I haven't used her half as badly as she has used me.

I leave her alone in the tower and go out into Sanctuary. The night is red with the Lake's unquiet glow. There are still many people moving through the ghosts in the levels of the ancient city, in the relative coolness of the night. I see lights in windows, and hear shouts and laughter and screams. Some of the lights are phantoms, and some of the voices echo inside me. I hear Spadrin's last scream, and I stumble against a wall, clinging to the rough stone.

I push myself away and move on, passing through ghosts, watching buildings melt and reform like mutating tissue inside clouds of ghost-light. It is almost as though I am looking through time, seeing Sanctuary's history unfold, superimposed on reality. I wonder how many people actually live here in the present, and how many of them are sane. . . . I hold the trefoil briefly; let it fall against my chest again, touching it now and then with my fingers as I walk.

"So, pilgrim, did you get what you came for?" a voice asks me unexpectedly.

The sudden question almost throws me into Transfer. My mind stumbles and pulls itself together desperately. *Stop! Stop!* "Yes! . . . What?" I find myself staring up into Goldbeard's mottled face. "What do you want?" I glare at him, because his expression fills me with cold fear. I remember that he heard me tell Song I wasn't a sibyl. *But I am a sibyl.* . . . Slipping, slipping. *Concentrate! Stop.* I take deep breaths, mumbling an adhani; knowing that it's futile, but somehow succeeding anyway.

"I want what belongs to me—"

For a moment my floundering brain thinks he means the watch.

"—the solii."

I blink. "The . . . Song gave you your reward." I try to push past him, but he grabs my arm.

"A lousy diamond. Where's the solii?"

I have to stop and remember. And then I tell him.

His jaw drops in moronic disbelief, snaps shut again with fury. "I'll spill your guts and find it, pilgrim— " He shakes me. "Only . . ." He lets me go abruptly. "She says not to touch you. She says you belong to the Lake now." He stares at me, as if he is seeing the sweat-streaked designs on my face for the first time.

I nod, eager to make him believe it.

"You hear the Lake talk?" he asks. "You see the future and the past?"

"Does . . . does she?"

"Sure." He nods, and I feel a giddy wash of relief. *I was right.* The ghosts, the buildings, are not hallucinations . . . they're something else. . . . One less symptom, one more clue. "Do you see them?" I ask.

He laughs, and spits. "Nah. She's the sibyl, the one got power over the Lake. It has her, and it leaves us alone."

"What do you mean?" The more I know about Song, the more I will know about what she has really done to me.

He shrugs impatiently. "I told you. The Lake does crazy things. It sucks you up and spits you out some other time. It makes things change so you can't find them. Look around here— " He waves a hand, covering an arc of jumbled ruins. "Only here it's better now, since the Lake has her. She takes care of us." He strikes his chest with a huge hand. "And I take care of her. I get rid of anybody who tries to do anything wrong with her." His eyes gleam with fanatical promise. "But she said let you alone . . . for now."

"What does it want with her?"

"You tell me!" he snorts. "You tell me, pilgrim. What does it want with you? What does she want with a limp one like you? Did she have you?" He stares me up and down, eyeing the painted whorls that cover my skin. Echoes of lust and sudden shame burn inside me, fire and ice.

He reads the answer in my face, and his own face fills with sullen envy. His hands clench. Even he is afraid to touch her. . . . And now I recognize the real source of her power. Her magic is just a game; even her sibyl's blood is nothing but a symbol. All her power over them lies with the Lake, in her control over it. But Goldbeard doesn't understand the Lake's power any more than I do.

She said I'm the one who was supposed to understand. But I don't understand! I feel my concentration dissolving like bubbles in an undersea swell of futility. There is someone else I need to ask Goldbeard about, something else I need to know. And he can tell me, if I can just hold on. . . .

By the time I recapture my drifting consciousness he is gone, and I am standing alone inside a crowd of rattling blue ghosts. They hover in the air; they seem to be doing something technical . . . I can't find the strength to wonder what it is. I push through them as if they aren't there, and move on aimlessly into town.

She said I'm the one; but I'm the wrong one. She's crazy— and so am I. The hopelessness of everything numbs my brain. I only want to forget. . . . I let my mind wander, until somehow I am reliving scenes from an Old Empire romance that I read long ago—the story of the first sibyl who ever lived, of how she survived in the days of the Empire's fall. The daughter of bioscientists, blessed and cursed by the divine madness that was the legacy of her murdered parents, she was lost on alien worlds, victimized by the family she thought she could trust . . . with only one true friend in the entire galaxy, one man who loved her and knew she was not insane. And she believed he was dead. . . .

I blunder into a pile of rubble and fall down, ripping the knees of my pants, bruising my palms. The pain clears my head, and I swear with disgust. Stupid, romantic crap—a book I left behind on Tiamat because I never wanted to see it again. I wonder why I even remember. . . .

Because she never gave up! my mind says angrily. She fought for her sanity, for her life, and she won. She saved herself, and the future. . . . *It isn't over yet. It isn't over until you surrender.*

I sit back against a pillar, holding on to the present with all my strength. I look up, focusing on the shadowed portico of the abandoned building. A dim finger of ruddy light points into the building's darkened interior, touching a wall of solid rock. There is no one inside, not even a ghost. I wonder what this place really was. . . . *What was this city?* Irrational pleasure fills me as I ask, and then uncontrollable frustration when I don't have the answer. "I should *know*! Why don't I *know*—?"

I grind my fists on the dusty tiles of the entryway until the seizure passes. And then, fighting to keep control, I begin to practice the rituals that Moon taught me. I force myself to recognize how similar the disciplines are to the adhani, just as she said. Perhaps they even have a common origin. The familiarity calms me, and slowly I begin to believe that I can make them a part of me, a shield against the chaos that is loose in my mind.

But as I let the belief take hold, a flood of irrational pleasure pours into me, sweeping everything away. "Moon!" I cry, "Moon—" I make myself remember the one person who still believes in me, the one person who still loves me. And blind passion becomes my love for her, genuine, measurable, real . . . a sea anchor, until reality resolidifies around me.

I slump back against the pillar, drained. What use is it to practice the sibyl litanies—? I turn the trefoil over and over with uncertain hands. They may save me from the Transfer, but they can't stop fits of manic depression from leaving my mind in ruins, every time I try to think rationally. And that is the difference between real sibyls and madmen. . . .

Every time— My mind prods me with sudden excitement. *Every time? Then the attacks fit a pattern.* I murmur an adhani, searching for the strength to follow one more thought through to its end. It is even harder to force myself to look seriously at something as repugnant as my own insanity . . . but I know that every time I have moments of lucidity, or discover another clue about what has happened to me, I feel obscene pleasure. And when I fail I feel suicidally helpless. Rational responses wildly distorted, beyond my control . . . because something alien is controlling me. Something far stronger than I am; something that also causes phenomena only a sibyl can sense. Chaos incarnate is driving me crazy, like a question without an answer. *But it wants me to win. It thinks I can.* It rewards me with pleasure when I try, and punishes me when I fail . . . *operant conditioning.*

I start to laugh, certain that all of this is only my own pathetic paranoia. Lunatics always think they're sane. . . . And yet, ever since Song infected me there *has* been an alien presence in my mind, wrapped around my thoughts like a brainprobe . . .

always the strongest, the worst, when I see Fire Lake. *Fire Lake. Can it possibly be alive . . . sentient?*

Exultation answers me. *But how? Why? Some unknown life form . . . is it really possible?* I get no response. Hope is real to me again, and with it, failure. But I know that whatever happens from now on I can only go forward, until I find the answer to this mystery, or die trying. I am a sibyl, and whether I am fit to be one or not, that change is inescapable, and permanent. And somehow it has bound me to Fire Lake. . . . I feel stronger in my new knowledge, and helplessly elated, and terrified.

I get up, restless with nerves. My feet lead me through the town until I find myself standing at the edge of the canyon again. I wonder fleetingly why I always seem to find myself here, where there is nothing. The depths lie in black shadow, but I hear the water chuckling over secrets far below. Looking down from the brink I see a faint glimmer of light pulse and fade. I remember that once I saw something silvery in the water's depths. Something about its shape was familiar . . . but there is nothing to see in the blackness. I look across at the quarter of the city that lies on the far rim, see it flickering with ghost-light, images winking in and out. There are no real people, no real lights there at all. The outlaws stay close to Song, under her protection. *But why? Why does the Lake need her, or me? What does it mean?*

I have too many pieces to a puzzle, and nothing to fit them into. I press my face into my hands, feeling my thoughts drown in noise. Moments of sanity are not enough. . . . Defeat weighs on me like iron. *I'm tired . . . I'm so tired of trying.*

I go back to Song's tower; not sure why, except that I have nowhere else to go. As I walk between the rows of bones I wonder suddenly whether she has ordered her guards to kill me. But I keep walking, and they let me pass. My tension grows as I climb the stairs to her chambers. The rooms are dark and silent. She is still lying on the bed, asleep now. The fire globe bathes her in dim, bloody light. She stirs as I enter the room, her face shadowed with exhaustion as deep as my own.

"Why do you let me live?" I ask dully.

"The Lake," she says. "The Lake needs you." She lets her head fall back again, lying passive and inviting on the silk and velvet coverings. "And I need you."

I lie down fully clothed—on the floor, where I will not even have to touch her. She murmurs a curse, and then is silent. I feel nothing but a cold knot of anger, and an aching loneliness.

When I wake again it is dawn. The town looks like burnished copper. I have been dreaming about my brothers; the memory jars me fully awake. Song is sitting on the bed with her knees drawn up, staring at me. I try to question her about my brothers, but she won't listen. She gets up and runs from the room.

Sitting on the floor, I realize that my body no longer hurts anywhere. I have healed overnight. *Overnight?* I feel only a passing dismay at the vagaries of time. I stretch without hurting for the first time in . . . longer than I can remember, and I am only grateful. I scratch at the sparse stubble of beard on my chin.

The Lake calls me to the window, and I look out at it. I watch it mutate and flow as it changes randomly, helplessly. . . . *Helplessly. How do I know that?* My hands make fists on the stone windowsill. I shut my eyes, reciting an adhani and feeling the demon choir inside me fade; listening for the darker voice hidden beneath them, the voice that I thought was my own madness—the voice of the Lake. I open my eyes, taking a deep breath, ready to try again.

How does this thing get into my mind? As I ask myself the question, I realize there can only be one answer: because I'm a sibyl, like Song. *But what is the mechanism?* I force my thoughts into the chains of question and answer. If I can only understand this, I'll know better whether I'm really insane—whether I can ever be sane again. *The virus causes altered brain structure, receptivity to a faster-than-light medium* . . . my excitement rises . . . *which means . . . which means . . .?*

"Shit!" I push myself away from the window as my concentration falls apart and the thing inside me gibbers its frustration. "Damn it! Damn, damn—" not even sure if the curses are my own.

Song cries out in the next room, as if she feels everything I do. I go into the room and she hurls a piece of clothing at me. "Get out! Get away from me, you failure, leave me alone!" Her voice is tremulous with pain, but her eyes are like obsidian. She clutches the fire globe against her breast.

"I didn't ask for this!" I snarl, sullen with exasperation. "I came here to find my brothers, not to solve your problems."

"Liar!" She stalks back and forth, her robe flapping open so that I glimpse a flash of breast or thigh as she moves. "You couldn't wait to get your hands on me. You wanted me—everyone wants me, because I have power. They'd do anything to have me. But they're all afraid of me except you." Her hands touch her breasts; I look away. "You weren't afraid . . . I thought you were different. But you're not the man who came here—"

"What do you want from me?" I shout furiously. "You infected me! You wanted a crazy man, and that's what you've got! Tell me what the bloody hell you—" I break off.

Her eyes are glazing . . . she has gone into Transfer.

"Song?" I stare at her. For a moment I can't even remember what question I've asked. And who have I called to answer it—

"Help . . . me," she whispers. "I want . . . help me. Order me."

The Lake roars into my mind, her voice echoes inside me, until I can barely speak. "Order—you to do—what? Who are you? Where are you?"

"Lost . . ." she moans. (*Lost lost lost.*) "Save me. . . ."

"Damn it—" I dig my fists into my eyes until I see stars. I know this is important, desperately important. But the Lake is all around me. "The Lake? Are you a prisoner of the Lake?"

"No . . . Lake. Here."

"Where? What—" I try to think. "What are you?"

"Lake. Lake." (*Lake lake lake . . .*)

My breath catches. The Lake is speaking to me, through Song. "But what *are* you?" I shout, shouting down the echoes inside my head.

"Your servant . . . Lake." Song's eyes are vacant, helpless.

I turn away, shaking my head, wanting to shake her. "How can I help you?"

"Ask . . ." she gasps, "ask the right questions."

What are you, what do you want from me, how can I help you—? "I can't think of anything else!" And unspeakable anguish fills me.

Song falls out of Transfer into a sobbing heap. "Please, please . . . !" she cries, as if her heart is breaking. "I can't . . . I can't . . . bear it. Help me—"

I fall on my knees beside her and take her in my arms, holding her against my heart, because her pain is mine, as bitter and unstoppable as tears. "I'm sorry, I'm sorry . . ." I groan, to her, to the raving monster that holds us captive. "I *tried.*" Seeing now that she is as much its prisoner as I am. "Why does it do this to you . . . to us? By all the gods, what does it want from us—tell me, Song!" I do shake her now, to make her listen.

She looks at me in fear, as if she thinks she will fall into Transfer again. "Don't!" I shout. She doesn't.

"It's so alone—" Her voice trembles. "There's no one else who hears it—not through a thousand years. So it keeps me here . . . I keep it here . . ." She wipes at her eyes. "It's lost in time. It *needs* . . ." She caresses the fire globe that lies in her lap.

"What?" I ask.

"You were supposed to know! You're supposed to . . . to *know.*"

"Why? Why me? Why not—Goldbeard, or somebody else? Why not you?"

"I can't! Nobody can answer it; nobody knows what it wants, nobody knows what it is! . . . I'm lost. I can't hold on to anything. It takes everything away from me. . . ." She clings to me, burying her face against my neck. Her whole body shudders. "It's eating me alive."

"Gods. . . ." I wipe my nose, sniveling with self-pity. I have failed again, failed miserably, and I don't even know at what. Why me? What do I know that matters? I'm no one— "I thought . . . I thought you controlled the Lake. I thought *you* knew what it was! I saw you with those men, you called up a power and you killed them—"

"The Lake killed them!" She pushes away from me. "It took them somewhere else. It touches the crowd through me. When it comes that close, *things* happen. Things used to happen to Sanctuary all the time, that's what everyone says. Until I came. Now they only happen when I can't hold on, when I hate them so much. . . ." Her hands clench. "I just never know *what*—"

"Were those men guilty?"

"I don't know." She looks at me strangely. Suddenly her fingers sink into my flesh. "I don't care! They're all guilty, those maggots! I suffer to save them—let them suffer too!" She begins to cry again, bruising her fists against my vest.

"Help me find my brothers," I say softly. "I know they're here. You even saw them, you passed judgment on them. Help me find them, and I'll take you away from here."

"That's not the answer!" Her eyes are like black glass again. "I know them, two Kharemoughis. They were worms, even the Lake didn't want them. So I let Goldbeard sell them."

I straighten up. "Who owns them? Where can I find them?"

"You don't want to know. That's not why you came. You don't care about your family. Nobody does, it's all a lie."

The words sink into my heart like a knife. "That's not . . . that's not true. My father . . . your mother—"

"I hate my mother! She never understood anything. She made my father feel like nothing, because he was . . . full of dreams. She never had any dreams. She never understood about being a sibyl. It was only a job to her. She let the Company use her and give us nothing. She was a sibyl, she could have asked for anything! But she wouldn't go somewhere where we could be rich and honored. She wouldn't listen to us—"

"Sibyls aren't supposed to want money or power," I say weakly, but she isn't listening.

"She didn't understand when I told her to infect me! She knew I was lying . . . but she did it anyway. And now she's sorry, but it's too late, too late. . . ." She wrings her hands. I realize finally that it wasn't World's End that drove her mad, but her madness that drove her into World's End.

Did mine? I climb slowly to my feet, staring out the window at the Lake. "I hate my brothers," I say thickly. "I don't know why I came . . . except that maybe I hated myself more." I turn back to her. "All my life, I always tried to do the right thing—but it always came out wrong." I'd been as self-deluded as any of the others back in C'uarr's place, the ones I'd despised for running away into World's End.

But this doesn't have to be the end of the world. "We can leave here, Song. Nothing's keeping us here. Tell me how to find my brothers—"

"You'll never leave here. Not unless you ask the right questions!"

"How?" I wave my arms. "What else can I try?"

She only stares at me, her face darkening. She gets to her feet suddenly and goes into the bedchamber with the globe in her hands. After a little I hear her call out the window to someone. I follow her into the other room.

She stands before an ornate mirror, holding a pot of red paint in her hands. She has put on the white shift I saw her wearing the day I came here, the day I saw the Lake kill the men on the platform. Looking at her reflection in the mirror, I see that the shoulder and neckline of the shift are torn; I remember that I was the one who tore them. I look away self-consciously as she glances at me. "What else is there to try?" I ask her reflection.

"You'll see," she says, gazing through me. She dips her fingers into the bright liquid, drawing swirls and lines across her face. I remember the patterning she wore when I saw her on the platform. I look down at the faded patterns on my own arms; finally I know how they got there.

I hear the tower door burst open, and heavy footsteps cross the floor of the next room. Suddenly Goldbeard is standing in the doorway. He looks from Song to me with morbid eagerness. "Him?" he asks, his hands flexing. "Now, Song?"

Song draws a leisurely line of red down her bare arm, and smiles. "Just hold him," she says softly.

I stand frozen, too stunned by the unexpectedness of this to do anything at all. Goldbeard moves behind me; his huge hands circle my throat and tighten. My own hands fly up in reflex, prying at his fingers.

"Don't," Song says. "Don't move, and he won't hurt you." She goes on calmly painting herself.

My hands drop, and the pressure on my throat eases. I take a deep breath, trying not to think. Fear leaves my mind too clear. Song comes toward me, carrying the pot of paint. She dips her fingers into the liquid again. She draws a line down my cheek, and then another. *Is this all?* I wonder dimly. But the paint has an oddly familiar consistency . . . a faintly nauseating odor. The color— A trickle of red drips onto the corner of my lip, and I lick at it with my tongue. A salty flatness fills my mouth.

Blood. I spit and gag, knocking Song's reddened hand away. Goldbeard's thick fingers close like a band of iron around my throat, crushing my windpipe until my ears sing, until my vision blurs and my knees buckle under me . . . and I stop struggling.

He holds me on my feet, letting me breathe again in ragged gasps, while Song smears me lovingly with blood. She repaints my face, my arms, my chest with dripping arabesques; I flinch like a wild animal every time she touches me. "Why—?" I say.

But she only answers, again, "You'll see." She picks up her red/gold cloak and puts it on. She goes out of the tower; Goldbeard follows her, dragging me along. Guards surround us as we reach the bottom of the steps; the canopy bearers materialize to shelter Song from the heat.

Song leads the procession down through her subjects and her ghosts and the morning shadows, as oblivious to one as to another. Goldbeard tosses out handfuls of coins, at her order, and people begin to follow us.

She takes the path along the canyon rim that leads to the fatal platform at the cliff's edge. A straggling mass of humanity trails us out across the plateau. When I realize where we are going I try to turn back, but Goldbeard and the guards surround me . . . and as we go on, farther and farther, an alien excitement begins to rise in me, overpowering my dread.

We reach the platform at last; I see it up ahead, hovering on the crest of that bloodred wave of stone. In my memory it is a wonder, a place of magic, hung with silken pennants. But what waits for me now is only a shabby raft of flotsam and faded rags.

We climb the trembling rope ladder—only Song and I, this time. Fire Lake is alive below me, murmuring, changing; mesmerizing. I feel my willpower dripping from me like sweat, until I cannot even be afraid. We stand together above the crowd.

"The Lake . . . the Lake calls . . . the Lake will speak to you." Song's voice is thin and reedy as she speaks to the crowd. Misery shimmers in her eyes. But she begins to sway, lifting up her hands, rolling her eyes like a phony occultist. She is an actor, giving them the performance they are expecting. People in the crowd start to shout questions at her—random, inane, absurd questions. I cover my ears with my hands.

Almost before I know it, she has gone into Transfer again. The questions stop, and she is answering . . . but her answers are as random and meaningless as the questions. She speaks in languages that I know and ones I've never heard of, reciting fragments of conversation, obscure bits of data, questions, complaints. This is genuine, I know; even as I wonder how it can be. The crowd stands silent with awe, and some of them actually kneel down. I feel the Lake's energy surge in the air around me. I thank the gods that there are no victims being offered up today, to be sacrificed to the terrible power she summons like a lightning rod.

Her possession goes on and on, agonizingly. My own mind grows heavy and dim; I stand gazing out at the surface of fire until my vision burns away and all I see are the phantoms that haunt my inner eye. The hot wind rising up the cliff face stuns me. I imagine myself melting, flowing down to meet the surface of the Lake. . . .

Song breaks out of Transfer again, falls forward against the platform rail. The crowd's roar of appreciation startles me out of my daze. Song straightens away from the railing, pushing her hair back from her sweating face. She raises her hands again, gasping for breath, to shout, "Is there a judgment? Today the Lake will judge you—through him!" She points.

She is pointing at me. "No!" I say. I try to run toward the ladder, but my feet turn me back again. My body belongs to the Lake now, not to me. I watch numbly as Goldbeard forces someone up the ladder to stand before me—two men, frightened and angry. They begin to argue, accusing each other: "He stole my slave—" "I won him fair—!"

I can't listen, I refuse to listen, searching for the strength to stop what Song is about to do to me. I cover my ears with my hands again as she cries, "What is the truth?" But Goldbeard jerks my hands down and pins them behind me. The two men back away from us, staring.

"Leave me alone!" I throw myself forward, using the pain of my twisted arms; I shout a sibyl litany—anything, to stop my mind from unraveling like a thread as Song asks the question again and again. I shut my eyes against the sight of the Lake but it burns its way through my lids. *No escape*—

"What is the truth?"

I sway . . . I feel myself letting go . . . and suddenly far below me the Lake passes through a spectral shift—*red* orangeyellowgreen *blue.*

I dissolve, flowing out into the Lake—not my body, but my mind. I am bodiless, infinite, exploding and reforming, disintegrating and reborn; here, there, now, then; boiling with a million memories that have no common ground. Chain reaction without chains, atoms of meaning fissioning into randomness and perversity. I am amorphous sentience, helpless, haunted, raging . . . tortured by loss, by the need for a time that was or would be: *For time flowing downstream, ordered, ruled, under control— Control . . . control . . .*

"Control!" I am shouting hysterically at the crowd. "Control!" I reel forward to the fence, gasping like a drowned man. The crowd shouts in meaningless exultation, while the Lake pours its maddening poison of frustration into me. *Why? Why?* I realize that I have seen the very heart of the truth . . . and still I do not understand. *What does it mean, what does it mean—?*

Then suddenly I remember the two men. I turn slowly, forcing my eyes to stay open. The two men are staring back at me, their own eyes glazed with fear—but they are alive, and whole. The Lake did not touch them. Somehow I have protected them. Relief leaves me limp. "Get out of here," I whisper, my voice breaking. They do.

I lean on the rail, stupefied and disoriented. When I begin

to care what is happening around me again, I see Song waving her arms, flaunting herself, flaunting her control over the crowd. Claiming all that has happened as her own doing. The sight fills me with disgust. But she throws me a look of hidden rage and anguish; she knows that I still don't have the answer. She uses me, like she uses all of them . . . but she's still a victim, just like I am.

I have to escape from this place. I go to the ladder and start down it. Song makes no move to stop me. Even Goldbeard seems to believe now that I'm possessed. I wonder if I shouted the same meaningless gibberish that Song did. . . . I stop in mid-air, clinging to the rungs. I know that I've heard those frag ments of random speech before. I still hear them, inside my head: the ghost-voices. Human voices. *Why is it obsessed with humans? What could we possibly mean to something so alien?* The Lake stirs, I feel its excitement expand inside me—I drop the last meter to the ground as I lose my grip on the ladder.

The mob backs away from me. I climb to my feet, and they make an opening to let me through. They watch me nervously, as if they expect the sort of theatrics from me that they get from Song. "Just stay away from me!" I shout. They seem more than willing to obey.

I walk back to town along the canyon's rim, solitary among a crowd of ghosts. The plateau is like an anvil under the hammer of the heat. I wish I had a sun helmet . . . I wish I had some shoes. I am barefoot—I only notice it now, as my bruised and bleeding feet stumble in the rocky path. But pain is almost a relief, by now, like hunger and thirst. Proof of my reality. I wonder how many performances like the one I just saw Song has put on for her subjects . . . and how much choice she has.

And how much chance do I have, caught between her and the

Lake? I rub my sweating face with unsteady hands. I have entered the Lake's mind, the way it enters mine. I have touched the heart of chaos. . . .

And it longs for order. The realization throws my thoughts together like clapped hands. *I was right all along.* It does want me to fight for control. It wants me to . . . *to order it.*

The Lake's elation screams inside me. I sink to my knees, fighting to hold my thoughts above water until it subsides. I get to my feet again, when I can, and go on.

How can I order the Lake? One human mind could never control a force so overpowering, even if it understood what it was controlling. *And I don't even understand that.* I look down into the purple-shadowed canyon, despairing—and see the unnatural glint of something silver far below. Waiting. Waiting. . . . I am back at the point where the canyons split. I stare down at the water, at the mystery lying in its depths. I don't understand why I am obsessed with this spot. Except that this thing is familiar, somehow. I've seen it before, somewhere. If I could only get close enough—

Suddenly I see—I *know* —where there is a narrow path that leads down the cliff face. My eyes spot tiny figures moving along the path, far below. I reach the head of the trail, and start down it.

The others who walk the trail are mostly carrying water, and most of them wear rags and chains. Captives from the wilderness. Slaves. I remember my brothers again suddenly, painfully. If they are still alive, this is what they are enduring. The slaves keep their heads down and avert their eyes when I look into their faces; trying to make themselves invisible.

I start to question one man about my brothers, but his face is utterly empty. I let him pass and stop another. He cringes against the wall and whines. I feel the yielding hopelessness of his body under my hands . . . my hands tighten instinctively until he winces. His fear makes me feel my own power; I want to beat him until he tells me what I need to know—

I release him suddenly, as if he is burning hot, and run on down the trail. When I reach the bottom of the canyon I fall on my knees at the river's edge and splash myself with water, scrubbing my body with sand until there are no bloodstains left on me. The water is ice cold; I bury my face in it and drink as though there is not enough water on the planet to quench my thirst.

Finally I get to my feet. I stand dripping at the water's edge and watch its undulating surface form impossible braids and patterns—defying gravity and my own need to see the river move like any river I have ever known. I try to believe that the water will not suddenly break its invisible bonds and drown me. The water murmurs and whispers, but the air is dead around me; there are no echoes falling from the canyon walls. I am alone here now, except for ghosts. A ghost haloed in red is chipping phantom stone from the steps at the foot of the path behind me. I hear her humming inside my head, and push her voice out of my thoughts with a conscious effort. *What are these people to you?* I ask the Lake, waiting for an answer I know will not come.

A flash of silver rises from the depths of the river as sunlight spills over the canyon's rim. It strikes me like the clear white light of revelation. I watch the sunlight turn the canyon walls to flame and illumine the river's blue-green depths. I see the silvery light-catcher clearly at last. It lies meters and meters deep, by the dark green mouth where water flows out of the hidden heart of the world to feed this impossible river. *Wreckage.*

I identify the pieces of twisted, broken metal for what they are, and my excitement rises. I move along the narrow stretch of shore, clamber up a pile of broken boulders for a better view.

The metal is old, corroded, eaten away by time and the river. Once there must have been more of it . . . a lot more. The river rolls and glitters and suddenly there *is* a lot more; I glimpse a crumpled form as large as—

The phantom is gone with another shimmer and twist of water, another blink of my eyes. I am not even sure that I saw it. . . . I'm crazy, I see ghosts—*Stop it, goddamn you! Analyze!* There is still wreckage in the water, but not all of it looks old. I force the wreckage of my thoughts to consider it again. There is a piece of hull . . . *a piece of hull.* Recognition is rewarded by a dizzying rush of bliss. I shake my head, throwing off the distraction. *A piece of hull.* I have seen that unmistakable form somewhere, but it fits no ship I have ever seen in the space-yards. And yet the metal looks new, now—*a trick of light and water.* There is something marring the perfectly preserved surface: symbols, lettering, words . . . but no language of any world I know. And yet, I *know* them. I strain forward; my sweating hands slide on the warm surface of the boulder. I can almost see it . . . almost see it in my mind. *Where have I seen this?*

Suddenly the memory bursts open, and gives me my answer: I see the university, the recording—the image opening inside my head again just as it did so many years ago. . . . The language is ST'choull. The language has been dead for a thousand years. And the ship is a Class Four Estade freighter of the Old Empire.

I slide down from the rocks, deafened by the ululation inside me. I fight myself for a space of clear thought; slowly it comes, and fills with more answers. A ship of the Old Empire crashed here. It must have happened during the Empire's fall, when refugees fled from world to world. Probably the survivors of the crash built the city up on the plateau. But then they abandoned it. . . . It has lain forgotten for centuries, lost in this heart of desolation. I frown. Why would anyone do so much here, build an entire city, and then abandon it? What could make them . . . *The Lake. Was the Lake always here?*

My body is wracked by ecstasy. I writhe against the stones as the Lake possesses and rewards me. *Stop . . . stop it! Leave me alone!* I plead. I claw my way back to reason; crouch strengthless at the foot of the boulders, gasping with helpless gratitude and frustration. "Who cares?" I shout at my demon. "Who cares about a dead city? Who cares why they left?" My frustration turns to killing despair, confusion; I feel my mind falling apart again. *Gods, I really am insane.* . . . I bury my face in my hands. *It's no use.*

"The clues were all there. They'd been there all along, of course," a voice says ironically; speaking in Sandhi, the language of my home. It is a very familiar voice.

I open my eyes. A ghost haloed in blue stands before me, with a face so familiar that for a moment I am dumbstruck by the sight of it. My father—as he must have looked before I was born. But then I realize that it is not my father . . . it is me.

Me—and yet a stranger, years older. A trefoil shines like a star among the medals and honors that crust my uniform. Seeing them, I seem to know when and where I was given each one, even though I've never seen them before. I sit watching as my other self goes on speaking, smoothly, with almost cynical ease—as I have never been able to speak before a crowd. He gazes not at me but through me, toward his phantom audience:

". . . though at the time I didn't consider myself lucky to be in the position. . . ." He smiles, but his eyes are hiding secrets.

I—he lifts his hands. There are no scars on his wrists. My heart constricts. He pauses, waiting for laughter. I hear the laughter inside my head, and wonder what I would see behind me if I turned to look. I do not turn to look. "I remember how I told myself at the start that someone would find the answer, if they'd only ask a sibyl the *right* questions. . . ." He glances down, grimacing at some private memory, and his face—my face—begins to fade.

"Wait! Wait!" I reach out, reach through him. "What questions?" My hand meets solid flesh, closes over an arm. I jerk back from the unexpected contact.

"BZ?" a hoarse voice murmurs in Sandhi. "BZ, is that you? Is it really you?" A familiar Kharemoughi face hangs before mine again—familiar, and yet profoundly changed.

"HK—" I whisper incredulously. I touch the face, and my hand confirms his reality. "HK!" I scramble to my feet, and grab him by the shoulders. "Holy Hands of Edhu! Ye gods . . . I never thought I'd find you alive."

He sags against me, his legs going out from under him, as if the shock is too much for him. I lower him to the ground and crouch down beside him. "You . . . you . . . what are you doing here?" he asks almost plaintively. "I hardly knew you."

"I came searching for you." It is almost too painful to keep looking at him. His once fleshy face is gaunt and haggard. His body is filthy and covered with bruises, his clothes are in rags. There is a metal collar around his neck, an oozing sore on his leg. I wonder morbidly how I must look to him.

"You came?" he asks again. "You came here to find us?" His voice rises. "You fool, you fool—you're the biggest fool of all!"

Irritation prickles inside me. His eyes catch on the trefoil dangling at my chest; he grabs it. "You told them you were a sibyl? Is that how you did it? When they find out, they'll kill you—" He drops the trefoil, his hands trembling.

"No they won't," I say, as calmly as I can. I grip his shoulders. "I really am a sibyl, HK."

"You? A sibyl?" His eyes focus on me again. "You said you couldn't . . . you never . . . How? When? Why?"

"Song. Song infected me." I look down, feeling my face flush, as if he could read how it happened in my eyes. "When I came here."

"Song!" His eyes bore into my head. "Then you must be crazy, just like she is!" He pulls away from me. "I saw you when I came down here, you looked crazy. You were talking to yourself—"

To myself. For a moment I don't realize that he means talking to the air. *Talking to myself. I saw myself . . . I saw my own future. And I will be—I am—perfectly sane.* I begin to laugh, for the first time in months, or maybe years. "I'm sane!" I grab HK again, shaking him, convulsed with laughter. "I really am, HK! It's going to be all right!" I realize that I am shouting into his cringing face, and try to control myself. I was right to believe in myself, right to go on struggling for my sanity, right to go on living— Relief and pride fill me, and are all my own. *I swear on my father's grave that I will never turn my back on the hard road again.*

"HK, listen to me," I say, more evenly. He averts his eyes; I make him look at me. "Something's happened to me, and I don't really know how to deal with it, that's all. But I'm learning. I'm going to be all right. Somehow it was meant to happen." I'd never wanted to be a sibyl, never even imagined I was fit to try . . . *but I am fit.* I take the trefoil in my hands again, feeling its treacherous beauty, barbed with pain. *Now, after all I've done . . . how is it possible?* I swallow the choking tightness in my throat, suddenly remembering the moment when I swallowed the solii, just before Song infected me. *Do you know the truth yet?* she asked me; and said, when I shook my head, *You will.*

HK sits watching me silently. I can't tell what he is thinking now.

"What about SB?" I look up, trying to convince us both that I am really thinking clearly. "Where is he? Is he all right?"

"All right?" HK's mouth twists. He scratches under his rags. I try to remember a time in our youth when I even saw him perspire. "SB is as all right as anyone here. He's a tool." His voice turns bitter.

"What's that?"

"A slave with special privileges. Anubah trusts him . . . and he knows enough about the equipment to make himself useful." HK's hands tighten into fists.

"What about you? You studied at the Rislanne—"

"I barely know how to use a terminal!" He glares at me. "You know that; you were always pointing it out to me. Do you really think Techs are born smarter than everyone else? Do you really still believe we were on top because we deserved to be?"

"No." I glance down at my wrists, and shake my head. "I'm not crazy anymore."

HK gets up. "You were crazy to come here," he says.

"Yes." I watch the water move. "I know."

"I have to get back." He picks up two pails and fills them clumsily at the river's edge. Somehow the water lies obediently inside the buckets. He stands looking back at me. "If you want SB, I'll take you to him." He starts away, limping. I catch up with him and take the buckets as we begin to climb the path. He leans heavily on my shoulder, until I can hardly keep my balance. My own feet leave a bloody trail behind us.

"HK," I say, "I'm going to get us out of here."

He looks at me bleakly. "Don't say that. Nobody ever gets out of here."

"We will," I promise. But the Lake stirs inside me, and suddenly I know that I will never leave this place alive, I will never be really free or in control of myself again—unless I solve the mystery that lives in my head, answer the riddle, ask the right questions. . . .

"You see?" HK mutters. "You know it too."

I don't answer. We reach the top of the cliff, panting and giddy from the pitiless heat, and start into the town. I try not to flinch as ghosts walk through me, hoping HK doesn't notice. *My own ghost* . . . I *did* see myself, safe and sane, in the future. All in blue. The way I saw my mother, in the past, in red. Song in red; my brothers in blue. As if I saw my own memories made into ghosts. . . .

But how can I remember things that haven't happened yet? How can I believe such a thing, how can I know that they aren't simply delusions? My confidence crumbles. *They're consistent!* my mind insists. Past and future are always consistent colors— *Why? And what about the rest of the ghosts—whose memories are they?*

Those things mean something together, they are too familiar. I stop in my tracks. *The Lake turned blue.* As I slipped into Transfer there on Song's stage, I thought I saw Fire Lake changing from red to blue. . . . *Time dilation.* The visual effects are like the changing colors of space seen from a ship approaching the speed of light. The universe shifted toward blue ahead, shifted red behind. The color of whole galaxies approaching or receding from our own at near light speed, in the infinity of space. . . . *What does time look like from the other side?*

Paradox. I'm living inside a paradox, time is flowing both ways— I feel ecstasy set fire to every nerve. *No, wait—*

"BZ! Goddamn it—!"

I am sprawled on the ground; I realize that HK has pushed me down. I sit up, shaking my head. I am sitting in a puddle.

"You spilled the water!" he whines. "You spilled it all, damn you! Now I'll have to go back down. . . ." He wipes his nose with his hand, mumbling.

I get up, wiping my hands on my pants, leaving rust-red smears of grit. I can't understand why he is upset, when my own problem is so much greater. "I'm so *close!*" My hands make fists. "I need a place to think and be quiet—" I look away, toward Song's tower.

"SB will kill me! You selfish . . . you spilled it. You go back and get more." HK waves his hand.

"What?" I blink at him.

"More water! SB wants it now. He'll—"

I stare him down, disgusted. "Just take me to him. He'll understand when he sees me."

HK's shoulders droop. He picks up the empty buckets and we go on through town. We reach the end of a wall that is half sheer rock; beyond it I see someone crouched in the scant shade of a doorway. I know who it is even before he raises his head.

"SB?" HK calls.

SB looks up. He wears a collar too. He has changed, but not as much as HK. He is clean-shaven; the lines of his face are harder, sharper than they were. A livid scar marks his jaw.

"Where the fuck have you been? What took you so long?" He gets to his feet, glaring.

"Look, SB, look—" HK pushes me forward like a shield.

"Who are you?" SB asks, but he is already staring at me. He half frowns. "BZ—?" He reaches out to touch me. "I don't believe it. You look like shit, little brother." He grins.

I nod, letting myself smile. "It's mutual."

"Ye gods," he whispers, as the realization registers. "You came here after us."

I nod again.

"And you didn't bring an army, the Blues—?"

"No." I shrug. "I barely got here myself."

"Wonderful," he says sourly. "And you always said the Child Stealer gave HK's brains to some lowborn. . . ." He picks up the thing he was working on when he saw us—a restricted tight-beam hand weapon. He tosses it at me; I catch it by reflex. "Here. I can't fix this—I've never even seen one before. You do it."

Old resentment twinges like a toothache, but I sit down and pick up his tools. "It's wonderful to see you too."

"What the hell do you expect? Are we supposed to be happy to see you trapped here like us? So we can all rot together?" SB looks up at HK again. "Where's the water?"

"BZ spilled it." HK shuffles his feet.

"Then go get more." SB points with his chin.

"I'm sick, SB. I'm tired. I can't. . . ."

"Let him rest, for gods' sakes," I say to SB. "It's hotter than hell."

SB ignores me. "Do you want me to tell Anubah you're too tired, again? That you're too sick to work for him anymore?"

HK's freckles stand out starkly pale against his skin. "No, SB. . . ." He glances nervously at the rug-hung doorway. "Is he inside?"

SB shakes his head. "He's with Gerth. And you know how he gets afterward."

HK picks up the pails and limps away with them.

SB watches him go, with a low smile.

I break open the butt of the tightbeam weapon and study its filaments through a magnifier. *He's your own brother!* My jaw clenches over the pointless words. *And both of you are still mine.* I wonder what I expected. I force myself to concentrate on the workings of the gun; my hands tingle with the Lake's unwanted pleasure in my competence.

"Why did you come?" SB asks me at last.

I look up at him. "Because I didn't have anywhere else to go."

He smiles the crippled smile again, looking for the scars on my wrists. "Did you think World's End would do what you didn't have the guts to do yourself?" He tugs at his collar.

I look down at my scars, and back at SB again, remembering the disdain in his eyes the last time we met. There are no scars on his wrists; none on HK's either. And suddenly the weals on my own arms are only healed flesh, nothing more. SB breaks my gaze. I snap the gun back together, and hand it to him. "There's nothing wrong with this. The charge is used up, that's all."

His frown comes back; he takes it wordlessly.

"Anubah—owns you?" I ask. The words feel awkward and ugly.

"Yes." I barely hear his answer. His fingers fumble with the gun.

I take a deep breath, shutting my eyes against a stabbing

memory of cages and pain. "HK said he trusts you. He trusts you enough to let you work on a weapon like that?"

SB laughs harshly. "As long as I wear this." He tugs at his collar again.

"A block?" I ask, looking at it with sudden recognition.

He nods. "If we try to use anything with a power charge while we're wearing this—" He makes an abrupt, brutal motion. "Anubah's got the control."

I shake my head. "Where the hell do they get something like that, here?"

"They trade for it, trade whatever they can find out there—trade for everything they can't steal off of poor bastards like us."

"With whom?"

"The Company." He shrugs. I raise my eyebrows. "Thousands of people work for the Company," he says, "and most of them barely get a living out of it. There are plenty who're willing to deal with real criminals, since they work for thieves already. At least this way they get their share."

I remember Ang, and I nod.

"You're not wearing a collar." He stares at me. "Are you free? How? Why?"

I show him the trefoil. "I wear this."

"A sibyl sign?"

I explain again, as briefly as possible.

He gapes at me, like HK did. "By all our ancestors, you're the last one I'd ever expect. . . . But you sound sane enough. Are you sure you're infected?"

I watch a ghost wander through him, and through the rug that hangs motionless across the doorway. The Lake stirs restlessly inside me. I laugh once. "I'm sure."

"Not everyone around here is afraid of sibyls. Some of them

really are insane . . . and some of them don't have enough imagination to go crazy, or to be afraid of anything either. Your luck won't hold forever."

"They don't touch Song." But I remember that she still keeps Goldbeard and a company of guards.

"Song!" He makes her name into a curse. "Everyone needs gods . . . especially in a place like this. If they don't have gods they invent them. They think she has power over Fire Lake— that her being here keeps Sanctuary from melting down and running into some crack in space."

"She does."

"What?" He snorts with laughter.

"She does communicate with the Lake. So do I. It's something to do with a sibyl's ftl receptivity, but I don't completely understand it yet. I see and hear things you wouldn't believe, since . . ."

"Shit, you are insane." He looks away. "And so is she. She's crazier than anyone here—or she's a better actor than anybody I've ever seen."

"She's both." I sigh, remembering the first time I saw her. "But she's trapped here just like the rest of us. And I swore I'd get her out—" I watch his face fill with disbelief "—just like I swore I'd get you out, and HK."

"Why, for gods' sakes?"

I stare at him. Finally I shake my head. "I wish I knew." I put out my hand. "Give me the gun."

He pulls back, his body tensing. "Anubah—"

"Tell him it was ruined. He trusts you."

SB grimaces. But then he nods, and hands me the gun. "If you can find a powerpack maybe you'll stay free a little longer, anyway."

"Long enough to get us all out of here." I fight down a wave of sickening self-doubt. "I will—!" I push the gun through my belt, covering it with my jerkin.

SB glances from side to side, his hands clenching. "Yes, by all the gods! You can do it, BZ. Get us out of here. We'll steal a flyer. We can do it now, before Anubah—"

"No. I have to . . . I have to . . . find . . ." I stumble over words as the Lake pours its anguish into me. "I can't leave yet . . . I have to find . . . I don't know *why* yet. . . ."

"What's the matter with you?" SB shouts. He slaps me. "Goddamn you, forget about Song. We're your brothers! She's nothing but a lunatic."

I climb to my feet, rubbing my face. He grabs at my clothes as I rise, trying to hold on to me. I jerk free as HK comes up behind me. HK stops uncertainly, his face running with sweat. Suddenly the watch begins to chime in my belt pouch.

"My watch," HK murmurs, when the chiming stops. "You found my watch." He reaches out, pawing at my belt. "Let me see it. Let me have it—"

I slap his hand away. "You lost it. I got it back. It's mine now." I look down, touching the pouch. "It was never yours to begin with."

His face crumples. "But it was all I had left."

"You've still got your life." I glance at SB. "I'll be back. I've always done my duty."

I make my way through the tumbled, stone- and rubbish-choked passages between buildings, out into an open square where I can get my bearings. I start upward, climbing ladders and steps, toward the heights where Song's tower lies. I will go there and wait for her. I try not to think about what will happen then; afraid of the Lake's response, when it knows my every thought. . . .

I turn a corner and collide with another body; curses wrench me back into the present. "You son of a bitch—" the stranger says. He breaks off, shaking his head. "Whose are you?" he says, his eyes narrowing as he looks me over, and doesn't see a weapon. His voice is slurry with drink or drugs; his eyes are bloodshot.

For a moment I don't realize what he's asked. "I'm nobody's . . . I'm a sibyl." I touch my trefoil.

His face turns greedy instead of afraid. "Then I can use you."

"I belong to the Lake!" I say. "I have Song's protection."

"She didn't tell me that." He laughs, and there is a knife in his hand. He flashes it at me almost carelessly. "Come on, pilgrim." His other hand closes over my arm, twisting it.

I bring my knee up into his groin; he bellows with pain and drops the knife. I break his grip on me and pull the beamer out of my belt.

He stares at it stupidly, as if I'd done magic like Song. I am a victim, a slave; he can't believe that I am defying him.

I pick up the knife. "I'm doing you a favor," I say, before he can start to think. "I told you I belong to the Lake. I could have torn you apart—"

He frowns uncertainly, still hunched over with pain.

"Come after me and I will," I finish, telling him something I'm sure he'll understand. I turn my back and walk on, trying to listen through the muttering of my voices for any motion behind me. But he doesn't follow. As I put another block of buildings between us I begin to breathe again. Now I wear the gun and the knife openly, as well as the trefoil, realizing that SB is right—my luck is running out. I walk faster.

I hide the gun again as I reach Song's tower and see the guards. The avenue of bones and the entrance with its leering skull sicken me. I can't believe that once I walked this path eagerly—and yet the memory lies as deep and perfect as a solii inside of me. I pass the guards. Their eyes follow me up the steps one more time.

Song has already returned. She stands at the window of the tower, staring out at Fire Lake. She doesn't seem to hear me as I cross the room to her. I touch her arm, say her name softly, trying not to startle her.

She turns, blinking at me, and her eyes are red with weeping.

"What is it—?" I begin. But I already know: the helplessness, the terrible sense of loss and futility—the Lake, which eats away at our wills, never leaving us alone. I've barely been able to survive it for this long, even with the adhani and Moon's guidance; but she has no control, no protection at all. How long has she endured this torture? How long has she waited for someone who could end it?

"Song," I say again. "I've found my brothers. We can all leave here now." I realize that she can make it easy for us; no one will touch her, or disobey her.

But her eyes fill with terror. "No! I can't leave the Lake. . . . Why don't you *save* me?"

"I will—"

"You're lying. You want to leave here."

"And take you with me!"

"No! You don't understand anything!" She pulls away from me, distracted, and moves across the room. When she looks back again her eyes are smouldering and unreadable. "Yes, I'll come. But I want you to bring something for me."

I nod encouragingly, and she points through the doorway into the next room. I go to the doorway to see what she wants.

"Over there," she says, "the fire globe." I move forward, and she shoves me into the room. The door slams behind me.

"Song!" The door is locked, of course. I beat on it with my fists. "Don't do this to me! Open the door, goddamn it!" The door is made of metal—*Ship metal,* I think irrelevantly—and I bruise my hands. I can see her through the filigree work of an inset panel.

"Stay there!" she cries. "Stay there until you save me or you starve!"

I kick the door and turn away, swearing furiously at her, at my own gullibility. I go to the window and look out, and down. The tower sits on a ledge of rock; the fall would kill me. I look up again, and the Lake is watching me, winking its many-faceted eyes at me, eyes that look forward and backward through time. "What are you, you souleater?" I shout. "Are you alive? Are you some kind of alien?" But those are not the right questions, and the voices in my mind scream the gibberish of the ages. "Then damn you!" People stare up at me. I pull back from the window.

And my father is standing before me in the room, haloed in red.

I gasp and fall back against the sill, wiping my hand across my mouth. *His ghost.* "F-father?" I ask, and wait for him to tell me what he wants.

"Thou are all I have that makes me proud," he says. His hands reach out to me. His eyes beg me to understand what he cannot ask, will not say. . . .

"Say it!" I shout, raw-voiced. "Say it this time, for gods' sakes, you coward! Goddamn you, you coward, you coward—why did you blame me? It was your duty, not mine! *Yours,* yours, yours. . . ."

I slide down to the floor, into a pile of clutter, hurling things across the room, hearing them shatter. *It wasn't my fault. It wasn't.* Feeling the pressure released, the pain ebbing away, the abscess draining in my soul. . . .

"Gods, Father. . . ." I murmur at last, slumping back against the cool stone of the wall. "The answer was so easy then." I pull myself up, and take deep breaths, reciting an adhani to focus myself. To find the right answer, you have to ask the right questions. Talking to the Lake is not so different from the Transfer, after all. Pushing away from the windowsill, I begin to pace off the small clear space at the center of the room. I count my steps, I measure the limits of my prison, I force my mind to grow calm and rational. I've spent my whole life running away from this moment. This time I will face the problem and find the answer, or else this time it really will be the end.

I realize that I need something to help me hold on to my clues if the Lake makes me lose control again. For the first time since I have come here I remember my belt recorder. I switch it on. It still works. I shudder as I hear my own last words. I advance it. I begin to record the data I have gathered, the pieces that almost fit; speaking aloud, afraid to imagine what sort of static it would register if I tried to use thought-record.

What have I seen? I count the anomalies on my fingers: "Relics of the Old Empire; a ship. Electromagnetic distortion. Space and time distortion. A river that ties itself in knots; buildings cut in half by pieces of stone; things that defy all reason, and yet must be real. . . ."

What do I feel? Helpless anticipation pours into me; I slam the floodgates of my concentration with all my will. "Emotions not my own. Images, ghosts—memories out of the past and the future . . . somehow. It all seems tied to a sibyl's receptivity; only a sibyl experiences these things, this sensitivity to the Lake."

What is the common denominator? I sink my teeth into my fist, holding on to the thought as the Lake's excitement rises. I see a pattern, an undeniable pattern: "The ship! The ship is the key, the ship that crashed here traveled faster than light. The Old Empire had a stardrive, bioengineered to manipulate space-time . . . an artificial intelligence."

I run back to the door, clinging to the tracery of metal vines. "Song!" I shout.

She turns away from the window, her body taut with anticipation.

"What formed you?" I watch her fall almost eagerly into Transfer. The Lake rushes into my mind; I keep shouting questions. "Was it the stardrive from the ship that crashed here? Is it still alive—?"

"Yes . . ." the Lake whispers, echoing, echoing in my head. "Lost . . . lost in time . . . buried alive! Your servant. . . ."

My vision, my hearing, are ablaze with phantoms. At last I understand the Lake's obsession with humans—its creators, its gods.

But it drove them away. "Why did you destroy this city? Why do you cause chaos in World's End?" The stardrive was designed to do one thing only: to manipulate the space-time continuum, to permit timelike movement by a ship through space without paradox. It could never be allowed to act on whim, or it would catastrophically disrupt human civilization. It was by definition a creature of perfect sanity and control. *But it acts randomly, unpredictably . . . insanely.*

"Order," the Lake whispers. "Lost . . . lost . . . order me!"

Torment shakes my mind. Order, disorder, madness—*why?* What trauma had it suffered. . . . *Of course.* "The crash!" I gasp, hanging on to the door, hanging on— "The crash damaged you." The crash must have destroyed its sense of order, turned its space-time interactions random. Its ability to maintain its own physical integrity had become uncontrollable mutation. . . .

Until now there are countless separate states of potential order, each functioning in its own reality, altogether. Together they breed madness, helplessness, despair—a tortured mind. *Fire Lake.*

"I understand!" I whisper. It has waited for its creators to hear it, to heal it, to give back its reason for existing. . . .

And at last, after a thousand years of waiting, someone has answered. I have. I am the right one, the one who knows, after all. I press my forehead against the metal filigree, supported by the solid reality of the door. "I know what you need."

"Yes!" Song screams with the Lake's voice. She turns from the window, I see her reaching out to me, tears running down her cheeks . . . but it is not her face that I see, it is Moon's, as the Lake enters my mind to reward me.

I stir on the floor and sit up. I shake my head, grimacing, wondering how much time has passed. It is night outside, but that means nothing, here. I wonder why I am still even trying to keep track of time.

The Lake. . . . I pull myself up the door until I am standing, barely. My body is rubbery and weak from hours lost in the Lake's rejoicing. I run my hands uncertainly over my stained clothing, to be sure all the parts are still there; look down at myself, but not too closely—knowing, but not ready to remember too much. I laugh, and there is still an edge of hysteria on it. I think that I will never be afraid of letting go, of losing myself in too much sensory pleasure, again . . . because nothing in human experience could possibly equal what I have just been through.

Aftershocks and afterimages spark and smoulder in my burnt-out nerve fibers, but my mind is clear enough to think again. I stagger to Song's bedside table through the ember-light of her fire globe. I look at the globe closely for the first time, and realize at last that it holds a captive droplet of the Lake itself. I touch it with uncertain hands, feeling its heat dimly through the heavy protective surface; feeling the Lake lapping inexorably on the shores of my mind. I unstopper the brandy and take a long drink. The liquor burns in my throat, making me cough, but feeding me strength. When I have enough strength to move again, I go back to the door. It is still locked; Song never reached it before the Lake overwhelmed us both. "Song?" I call, but she doesn't respond. I can't see her in the darkness beyond.

After some searching I find a light panel, and turn lights on in the room; realizing that somewhere here there is actually a generator. I begin to search through Song's piles of treasure. There must be something in this warehouse of contraband with a powerpack I can use in the beamer.

I find my desert boots, wince as I pull them onto my swollen feet. And at last I find what I am looking for—a broken module off of some unlucky pilgrim's rover. I jam one of the oversized packs into the gun butt, hoping that it still has enough of a charge to do me some good. I aim the gun at the lock mechanism on the door. I shut my eyes against the glare and press the firing button down for a count of ten. When I open them again, there is a glowing hole in the door where the lock used to be. I kick the door open.

I see Song lying on the floor, in a wash of light. I go to her and touch her throat, feeling for a pulse. She is alive, just unconscious. I sit down beside her, relieved.

But it is night. I decide that now is the best time to try to get out of here. I shake her gently, but she doesn't stir. I bring the brandy and let some trickle into her mouth. She coughs and swallows convulsively; her eyes blink open.

She stares at me, astonished. Her astonishment changes

slowly to comprehension, and a shining peace. "BZ . . ." she murmurs, "you understand!" I nod, smiling a little. "I never thought you would—I never thought anyone would. . . ." Tears well up in her eyes; she buries her face in her ring-covered hands.

"Song," I say, pulling at her elbow, trying to get her to her feet, "we're not out of this yet. But we can leave here, now."

"Leave?" Her face fills with terror. "No! I can't leave—"

And all the helplessness, the dismay, the terror, that I thought I was free of rolls back into my mind. Every possible thing that could go wrong if we escape flashes across my inner eye, paralyzing me. "But I understand!" I shout. "It's not fair!" I grab Song by the shoulders. "What the hell do you want from me—?"

She falls into Transfer, and the Lake moans, "Need you . . . need *you* . . . order me. . . ." Suddenly I see that understanding is not a cure—recognizing insanity does not heal a twisted mind. It needs more . . . more than we can ever give it.

"I can't heal you!" I say the words to Song. I think of how helpless I am here, helpless to save the Lake, to control it, to give it what it really wants. "I can't heal you. Song can't. There are people who can—" People who had understood the technology for centuries, lacking only the raw material to make it work. "Those people would sacrifice anything for the knowledge I have in my head! But I have to tell them! If I stay here I'll die, and the truth will die with me."

The helplessness and terror surge inside me . . . and fade. Song shudders and falls back into herself, lying limp in my arms. I have made it understand. I take a deep breath and get to my feet, thanking a thousand ancestors . . . the ancestors who created the technology of the Old Empire. "Come with me," I say gently. "It's all right now." I take her arms, trying to lift her up.

She slides out of my grasp, shaking her head. "No."

"But you hate it here; you hate what the Lake is doing to you—"

"It needs me. It's alone, it needs me. I'm important here, I'm a queen! I belong here, I want to stay—"

"Goddamn it," I shout, losing all patience, "you're crazy! You need more help than the goddamned Lake does, and I'm going to see you get it. Come on—" I jerk her to her feet.

She pulls away from me, and begins to scream. I hit her; the scream stops and she slumps to the floor.

I go to the door and shout down to the guards. "Something's happened to Song!" They come running up the steps, their guns out. I hit the first one with a chair as he starts through the doorway, and knock them both back down the steps. They don't come up again.

I start to pick up Song; stop, and go back into the other room. I take the globe that holds the droplet of Fire Lake. I fold it in a piece of heavy cloth, and tie it to my belt. Then I wrap Song in a dark rug and carry her over my shoulder down the steps.

We leave the skeleton tower unchallenged, and I search for a way back through the treacherous light-and-shadow alleyways of the town. I get lost half a dozen times before I find the place where I left my brothers, but nobody I meet is crazy enough to challenge an armed man carrying a body.

I hesitate when I reach the doorway that I think is Anubah's. The rooms inside are dark, but a group of men is laughing and gaming a little way down the alley, by the light of a solar torch.

A figure emerges from the doorway, and I stiffen.

"BZ?"

"SB!" I start toward the door, but he holds up his hand.

"Quiet, Anubah's inside, sleeping." He gestures me down

against the building wall. "Thank the gods," he mutters. "I thought you were never coming back."

"I said I always do my duty."

He frowns. I lay Song down beside me as carefully as I can; sit back against the wall, with my arms and legs trembling. I wonder dimly how long it has been since I've eaten anything.

"Is that her?" SB asks.

"Yes."

He grunts something that sounds like "Idiot," and turns to the doorway again. "HK," he whispers.

HK emerges, carrying a small case. They crouch down beside me. "Here are the tools." SB takes the case from HK's hands. "Get these blocks off us. Can you short them out?"

"Not if you want to keep your heads. Can't you get the control box?"

"No. I don't know where Anubah keeps it—" He breaks off, lowering his head as someone strides by.

When the stranger is past, I say, "I've got the gun working. Let's just get out of here."

"No! I want this off. I want to leave here like a man, with honor." He grips my arm. "You understand." His eyes burn holes in the darkness.

"All right." I pick through the tools in the dim light reflecting off the walls. "It's too dark here . . . wait." I unwrap the fire globe. Its restless glow washes their faces with warm radiance.

"What is it?" HK whispers. "Lava?"

"A drop of Fire Lake." I look up, grinning with elation. "It's stardrive, HK! The whole damned lake!" The real significance of my discovery is only beginning to penetrate.

"What are you talking about?" SB snaps. "Shut up with that crazy talk, and get us free."

"I'm not crazy." I meet his eyes. "I've discovered what Fire Lake really is. A ship of the Old Empire crashed here, and nobody knew it. Its drive has been breeding here, uncontained, for a thousand years. That's what causes all the abnormal phenomena. Think of it, SB! Think of what this will mean to the Hegemony!"

"You're sure?" he asks. "You're sure?"

"Absolutely."

"Gods . . ." HK sighs. "And we're the only ones who know."

"All the more reason to get out of here alive." I switch on the magnifier, and watch the invisible tracery of the blocks' circuits glow on its surface. I follow the microfine pathways inward more by instinct than by sight. "All right! . . . Give me a tone box." HK puts it into my hand. I press a code sequence—half audible notes, half silent to my ears. The pinprick red lights on both their collars wink out. "Deactivated. You're free. Now come on, let's—"

"One more thing," SB says grimly. He picks up the beamer before I realize what he is doing, and disappears through the doorway. I curse. "What's he—?"

A bellow of fury, a low voice speaking. A flash of light, and a scream—

The men down the alleyway look up as SB bursts out through the doorway. Some of them start to get up, or call out Anubah's name.

"Now I feel like a man." SB grins at HK, holding up the gun.

"You killed him?" I whisper.

"Sure." He nods. "He deserved it."

I look away mutely, too many voices in my head.

"Gods, SB," HK whines too loudly, "they know what you did!" He points down the alley, jittering with panic.

"Quiet—" I mutter, but he grabs the fire globe and begins to hobble away. Someone shouts at us. SB's arm comes up with the gun. "No!" I say, but he fires wildly. I see weapons come out, and the others start for us in a mob. I pick up Song and we all run. She is a dead weight, but rage at my brothers gives me more strength than fear does.

The twisting alleyways, the maze of steps and ladders, are our enemy and our friend. As we run I fix an image in my mind of the landing flat, the waiting rovers—*escape, freedom*—willing myself to see them ahead.

And abruptly I do, almost as if I have the power to twist time and space. With the last of my strength I run out onto the field. But in the hard glare of the lights I see more outlaws, and Goldbeard, roaring, pointing at us—

"There! He has her! He stole Song!"

SB fires at him and Goldbeard crumples, but the rest come toward us in a raging mass.

"Leave her, drop her," SB gasps, pulling HK by the arm. "It's her they want! They'll tear us apart!"

I run for the nearest rover instead, and drag Song's body on board. SB and HK throw themselves through the doorway after me. I seal the door, and fumble the remote into my ear. I gasp an override command, collapsing into the pilot's seat. The control panel comes to life. I lift off, hearing HK and SB grunt as the takeoff dumps them against the back wall. I can barely keep my leaden hands on the controls as we rise from the plateau into the darkness.

Song stirs at last, lying beside me on the floor. Whimpering in confusion, she pulls herself up the panel to look out into the night over Fire Lake. "No . . ." she murmurs. She looks at me and begins to shout, "No. No! Take me back!" Her fists strike the panel.

I ignore her, wiping sweat from my eyes as I count the images on the screen that are outlaw flyers on our tail. This rover is too old, too slow, too clumsy, to outrun them all. And if they force us down . . .

Song begins to shriek hysterically. My head fills with noise, with the wail of a thousand memories . . . with a blazing explosion of energy. Below us the Lake explodes in sudden gouts of fire. The rover reels and plunges as the shock waves batter it. And with dazzled eyes I see the plateau that holds Sanctuary shimmer, see it begin to crumble—see it flash out of existence, as if it had never been.

But my disbelieving eyes still show me our pursuers below, closing, closing. . . .

I shut my eyes and concentrate on the impossible: a clear sky, no pursuit, a new day, with Fire Lake far behind us—

"No!" Song screams, one last time.

"What happened?" SB is shouting. "Sainted grandfathers what happened? Where are we?"

I sit staring out at a perfectly clear sky, darkening upward from palest blue to an indigo zenith. World's End flashes by beneath us, falling into the past. There is nothing on the screen. It is a new day. And the silence inside my head is deafening. The Lake is gone. "SB . . . take the controls. . . ." I lock the rover on course.

He slides into the seat as I get up. My legs give way; I have to hang on to the panel for support. I look down at Song, sitting rigidly in the copilot's seat. "Song?" Her eyes are open, staring, but she does not move. I shake her gently. She falls back into the seat, completely limp, still staring. "Song!" My own voice shouts in my ears. The Lake is gone, and the silence is almost unbearable. . . . *Gods, what have I done?*

"What the hell happened?" SB says again, pulling at my arm. "BZ—?"

"The Lake," I say, and for a long moment it is all I can say. "It let us go."

I feel them look at each other, and at me. "Then everything you said is really true," HK breathes.

"Where are we?" SB looks down at the readouts on the panel.

"On a course that will get us back to civilization in about half a day." Half a day's painless, normal flight. My hands touch my face. I feel a kind of amazement. We've survived.

"You mean the Lake is alive?" HK is sitting behind me. He holds up the globe, peering in at the droplet of stardrive.

I nod, relieved to see that he still has it.

"And you can talk to it?"

"I did. In a way." SB looks back at me. HK stares with childish awe as I fall into a seat beside him. "I don't hear it anymore. I don't expect it hears me, either." I feel empty, bloodless. I glance at Song again.

"Thank the gods you didn't drop that." SB looks over his shoulder at the globe.

"Drop this?" HK shakes his filthy head, holding it up. "I'd die first. I'd kill first. Ye gods, SB, do you know how much this is worth?" He giggles. "Nobody knows how much it's worth! More than anyone ever dreamed! We found our treasure." He peers out at World's End. "The hell with buying back the family holdings. We'll buy whole planets!"

SB laughs. "We'll sell it to the highest bidder. We'll *rent* it. We'll have the Prime Minister on his knees, begging us for our secret—"

"We'll buy the water of life! We'll live forever!"

I push myself up. I reach out and take the globe from HK's

hands. It whispers faintly, comfortingly. "Aren't you forgetting something?" I ask.

They look at me blankly.

"This is my discovery."

"BZ—"

"You can't—!"

Their voices clamor in the tight space of the cabin, rattling off the walls.

"—selfish—"

"—all we've suffered—"

"—share it with us?"

"We deserve it!"

"Shut up." I glare at them. "The stardrive belongs to the people of the Hegemony. It's their heritage, their right. And I'm giving it back to them. No one is going to hold it for ransom."

"You're going to *give* it away?" SB says scornfully. "You can't be serious."

"I've never been more serious in my life—" I blink and frown as life echoes memory. . . . *Just the way I saw it.* The last shadows of doubt about my sanity begin to fade. I move back to Song, and hold the globe in front of her eyes. "Listen," I beg her. She seems to focus on it, but she doesn't move.

SB watches us. "She got what she deserved, at least."

"But BZ . . ." HK's voice paws at me. "What about the family estates? Don't you want them back? Don't you want—"

SB snarls at him, and he stops talking. SB looks up at me. "You'll change your mind."

I shake my head.

We make the rest of the journey in complete silence. The silence in my mind is far worse. The thoughts that should have come to fill the emptiness refuse to form. I remember Ang and

Spadrin, see my brothers in their place; but I have no strength left for guilt, or pain, or even irony. My exhaustion is so utter that I can't even sleep. I watch the wastelands replaying and receding: the deserts, the mountains, the jungles . . . the greed, the suffering, the lost dreams. Only the prospect of seeing the Company town again makes me feel anything—an eagerness I never dreamed I'd ever feel, because this time it marks the gateway out of hell.

It is the middle of the night when we land at the Company's field. The agents search us with grueling thoroughness; but they can't prove we aren't what we claim, and even they have some respect for sibyls. HK and SB watch me tensely, but I am not about to give my secret to the Company. The globe is tossed aside as a useless curiosity; I pick it up again as soon as the agents leave the rover. They impound our vehicle, knowing we don't dare complain. We'll never see it again. But it doesn't matter. We are free, and safe.

I lead Song as we leave security; she follows me docilely, her eyes on the globe. I look for her mother beyond the gates, somehow expecting that she will know to meet us there; but she doesn't. I want to ask where she lives, but SB and HK insist that we book passage back to Foursgate before I begin my search. I give in, because I want to believe we are really getting out of here as much as they do.

People gape at us as we walk through the Port Authority buildings. I am beyond caring what anyone thinks; my credit is still good enough. The first shuttle that will take us back to Foursgate does not leave for a day and a half.

We eat a real meal at the port, ordering enough food to make the table creak. Song does not touch hers. As I listen to my brothers' endless, whining attempts to change my mind about Our Treasure, my own ravenous appetite shrivels and my stomach tightens around a lump of cold contempt. I pick at my food, ignoring them, until at last they stop speaking. Their eyes watch me with sullen speculation. They mutter to each other words I can't make out.

At last SB says, "Well, if you're going to get rid of her"— gesturing at Song—"let's get it over with."

I nod, surprised, and we take her back into town. It is mid-morning already; a hot mist clings to us as we walk. I am filled with an eerie sense of déjà vu as we walk the white, shuttered streets. *Welcome to World's End.* SB roams ahead impatiently, asking for the sibyl. Most people won't answer him; I can hardly blame them. I follow more slowly, burdened down by my beaten body, by Song's lack of will and HK's complaints about his leg.

SB reappears from around a corner, just when I think we've lost him completely. "Down here!" he calls. "She's down here."

We follow him down the alleyway. We are in a part of the town I don't know at all, emptier and even more run-down than the rest of it. Unwholesome fungal life oozes out of cracks and crannies. SB leads us into a peeling courtyard. The buildings here look deserted. I can't believe Hahn is forced to live in a place like this. The instincts of long experience begin to jangle inside me, and I try to force my brain to function. "SB, this doesn't—"

"In here," he insists, holding open a door. "She doesn't want anyone to know about this."

That makes a kind of painful sense, and I lead Song forward. HK shuffles behind me. I search the room with a glance as we enter it, but there is no one else here. "SB, what the hell—" I begin angrily.

He shrugs. "We needed a place to have one more little talk about our future. HK, get the globe and bring it to me."

HK jerks the globe from my hand, and moves to SB's side. SB sits on the edge of a broken table. "Now, shall we go over the reasons why you're being an ass, again?" he asks me.

"I already told you, nothing you can say to me is going to change anything." I take a deep breath, trying to keep my temper. "Listen, SB, we've all been through an ordeal. I know what you must have suffered. You were out there a lot longer than I was. . . ." The words feel as cloying as dust. "But you'll see things clearly again when you—"

"When we what?" he says bitterly. "What do we have to go back to? Nothing, unless we have this." He points at the globe.

"Have you considered honest work? I rather enjoy it, myself."

HK sneers. "You hypocrite. You wanted the estates for yourself. You think we don't know that? The only reason you left home was because Father put you in your place."

I feel my face flush. "You mean I should have stayed, and helped you suck our ancestors' blood?" *I would have killed you first.* My hands turn into fists. I force them open again. "That— that doesn't matter now," I say weakly. "It's past, it's gone. What matters is that we're all the family we have left. This is stupid—"

"Then why can't we be rich again together?" HK says. "Why shouldn't we? Isn't there anything you want? There's got to be something—something you want more than anything. Something you could never have, that you could have now—"

Moon. Her face fills my mind. "Moon. . . ." I realize what I have not had time to realize until now—that the impossible has been made possible . . . that to see her again is possible, because of Fire Lake.

"You see?" SB says eagerly. "There is something! I knew you weren't so fucking pure. You can have anything you want; we'll share it, all of us—" Naked greed fills his face, and HK's. "There's more than enough."

"No," I say flatly. "Never." I realize there is nothing that could make me willing to give them that kind of power. "You don't deserve it."

Their faces freeze. I glance at Song, still standing vacant-eyed beside me and gazing at the globe.

"Then let me give you one more reason why you should do this our way, little brother," SB says. He reaches into his ragged coat, and brings out the beamer. "Because you want to stay alive."

"Father of all our grandfathers!" I move forward angrily, not believing for a moment that he means it. "I've had enough of this shit, SB. Give me the globe, and the gun, damn it." I hold out my hand.

SB doesn't falter; the gun stays steady in his hand.

I stop, looking from his bleak stranger's face to HK's. HK looks down, staring at the globe. My empty hands clench. "Come on!" I almost laugh. "You aren't going to use that gun. You aren't going to kill a police officer. You aren't going to kill a sibyl." I hold up the trefoil. "Damn it, you aren't going to murder your own brother—" I take another step.

SB fires.

Gundhalinu cursed softly, slumping back against the clear window-wall as the shock of betrayal doubled the agony of remembered pain. For a long moment he sat staring into the minutely familiar corners of his office, like an amnesiac who had suddenly recovered his memory. And at last he pushed himself stiffly to his feet, pressing his arm against his side as he made his way back to his desk. "Ossidge?"

"Sir." His sergeant's voice answered him in less than a heartbeat.

"I'm ready to see the prisoners now."

"Yes, sir."

He sat down in his chair, listened to his heart still pounding. The adrenaline was flowing again, with the memories. . . .

The memory of his brothers standing over him as he lay, trying not to weep or moan, while they argued about whether to shoot him again. The memory of HK stealing the watch from his belt pouch before they abandoned him to die. . . . The memory of lying for hours on the floor while nameless, unspeakable things crept unseeing across his face; in too much pain even to move, but exquisitely conscious of every passing second, the blisters rising on his skin, the smell of charred flesh, his life's blood spreading out in a shining lake around him. . . . Crying out for his brothers, for a passing stranger, for anyone in the universe but Song—

Song, who stood staring down at him mindlessly, an empty vessel. He had begged her to get help, to find her mother, someone, anyone. But she went no farther than the door; and then returned, to stare down at him again with fathomless eyes, while the hours passed like years.

Until at last he heard a voice calling Song's name; and like a miracle or a hallucination, her face was transformed into the face of her mother. "Hahn," he had gasped out, once, twice; so afraid that she would think he was already dead, and leave him there. . . .

"Gedda!" Hahn cringed away from him, her face stricken— looked at her daughter, back at him, her hands fluttering in the air. "Song! *Song*—?"

Song's face reappeared, suddenly alive with fury, her eyes spilling over with tears. She began to scream at her mother, incoherent accusations and protests. Her voice was an endless outpouring of desolation, sweeping away her mother's words of rising grief and anger. They struggled, hands flailing—fell into each other's arms, weeping, while his vision slowly filled with blood, and they became the voices of ghosts, as he was already a ghost to them.

When he opened his eyes again it was to the perfect whiteness of fields of snow . . . until his vision slowly cleared, and he knew the whiteness for a hospital trauma tank. Somehow they had brought him help, after all . . . though he knew from the silvery cocoon that surrounded him how close he had come to not needing it.

And then he had remembered *why*, and known what he had to do. He had dragged himself free of the life support, like a dead man rising from a coffin; bringing medical technicians on the run. He remembered them staring at him in laughable disbelief as he demanded the time of day, and then a comm link, and an identity scan—

He had proved his right to be obeyed, in the name of Hegemonic security. He had watched through a fog of pain and drugs as the staff obeyed, deferred, acted on his orders, all the while stealing glances at the readouts above his head. Their expressions told him they didn't know how he was even able to function.

He functioned because he had no choice, enduring drugs and pain as he had learned to endure the Lake. And slowly he came to realize that they obeyed him not out of loyalty to the Hegemony, but because of the trefoil they had found around his neck. Knowledge was the one true and lasting power. . . .

Gundhalinu felt for the trefoil resting against the smooth fabric of his uniform. *Knowledge.* He knew now, really knew, what it meant to be a sibyl. Not a saint, not a god . . . only a vessel. *Only human.* He clutched the pendant in his fist, remembering the moment when he had first put it on; his hand tightened, until he felt the barbs wound his palm again. Droplets of blood crept down his wrist into his sleeve. It was nothing like what he had imagined. . . .

A light blinked on his terminal, and he touched the board. The door to his office opened. Ossidge led the two prisoners into the room. Their faces were still obscured by security bubbles; they had been held incommunicado for nearly four weeks. They had been cut off competely from contact with the outside world from the moment of their arrest, on his orders. He had called it a matter of high Hegemonic security, blocking all their civil rights. He had been justified.

Ossidge stood waiting.

"You can remove their restraints, Ossidge. I'm going to interrogate them off the record."

"That's not regulation, Inspector." Ossidge stood like a lump of granite.

"This is an extremely . . . sensitive matter, Ossidge." The inspector who once would not have tolerated the smallest infraction leaned forward across his desk, willing Ossidge to yield—

Ossidge nodded. "All right, Inspector. Because it's you who's asking. I wouldn't do it normally, but since it's you . . ." He released the prisoners. He started for the door.

"Thank you, Ossidge," Gundhalinu murmured, surprised, until he remembered why the note of near-awe hung in his sergeant's voice.

Ossidge turned. "I just want to say something, Inspector. I think it's a rare piece, how you've come back to the force . . . I mean, considering you're about the biggest hero—"

"This is the only place I want to be, right now," Gundhalinu said gently, cutting him off. "This uniform feels better than it has for a long time." He smiled, but it was not the smile he would have liked.

Ossidge smiled, too, for the first time that Gundhalinu could remember. He saluted, and left the room.

Gundhalinu waited as the two prisoners slowly removed their helmets. He saw their faces clearly for the first time, and they saw his. Their faces registered a play of emotions so extreme that it almost struck him funny.

"You—?" "BZ!" The voices of his brothers merged into a cacophony of disbelief.

He sat motionless behind his desk, saying nothing. They looked like the brothers he remembered, again—clean, healed, civilized even though they wore prison coveralls. But he no longer trusted his eyes. "Hello, HK . . . SB."

HK dropped to his knees in front of the desk. "BZ, by all our ancestors, I never meant for it to happen! Thank the gods you're alive—" He covered his face with his hands. "I don't understand . . . I don't understand what happened."

"The hell you didn't," SB muttered. "You were counting credits right up to the moment the Blues picked us up."

"That's not what I meant." HK shook his head, looked up at his brother, scowling.

Gundhalinu got up from his chair, grimacing slightly as his side hurt him. He moved around the desk and put out his hands to pull HK up.

HK climbed to his feet—leaped back with a yelp of fear as he saw the blood on his skin, blood from his brother's hand.

Gundhalinu shook his head, smiling faintly. "You aren't contaminated."

HK rubbed his arm against the leg of his coveralls, but the stain did not disappear.

Gundhalinu leaned heavily against the desk edge, trying to catch SB's gaze.

SB looked down. "If you're waiting for excuses, I don't have any."

Gundhalinu sighed. "No, brother. That's not what I was waiting for."

SB's head came up slightly, but he only said, "I tried to kill you. I thought you were dead."

"I was close enough." His hand pressed his side.

"What happened?"

He almost thought his brother sounded aggrieved. "The powerpack was nearly out of charge." Irony pulled his mouth up. "World's End had the last laugh, after all. . . . Song's mother found me. Song showed her where I was."

"Song?" HK said stupidly. "But I thought she was—"

"They're mind-linked somehow, by the Transfer. She can make her mother share what she sees—" He broke off, as the memory of his time in the abandoned room blurred the present. "Hahn got me to a hospital. And I sent the order to have you arrested before you could get back to Foursgate and start blackmailing the Hegemony." *It all sounds so simple. Like a lie.* He watched his brothers' faces tighten and close.

"What did you do with the stardrive?" SB asked, finally.

"Just what I said I'd do. I turned the sample over to the Chief Justice, along with a full report." He could barely even remember the circumstances, anymore. After his coded call to the Chief Inspector, they had come to World's End and taken him back to Foursgate, into a hell of reconstructive surgery and questions, rehabilitative therapy and questions, interviews and interrogations and questions, questions, questions. . . . "My hypothesis has been confirmed."

Their faces turned as desolate as the wastes of World's End. "And what did it get you?" SB said bitterly, looking around the room. "Nothing."

"On the contrary." Gundhalinu smiled. "You didn't hear the sergeant—I'm quite a hero. They can't do enough for me. They're about to promote me to commander. I expect I could have just about anything I asked for, at this point." *And maybe I knew it would happen this way all along.* He watched their faces, and felt his smile turn to iron. *And that was why I could never let you be a part of it.*

"Then, why don't you take it?" HK said. "You said there were things you wanted. You're just like we are!"

"No," Gundhalinu said softly, "I'm not. But you're right, there are things I want. I've already gotten one or two of them. But most of the things I want just aren't that simple. They take time." *And planning, and patience. . . .* And the certainty that he could change the web of other people's manipulation that was already tightening around him; that he could make it into a ladder, leading him ever upward toward his goal.

"What about us?" SB asked.

Gundhalinu looked back at them almost absently. He folded his arms across his aching chest. "Well, I thought about charging you with attempted murder, and maybe treason."

"But we're your bro—!" HK bit his lips, his freckles crimsoning.

"'Blood is thicker than water'?" Gundhalinu smiled again, a rictus. "I know. I've seen a lot of my own lately."

"You still owe us something." SB sat down in a chair, his eyes glittering. "You'd never have gotten out of Sanctuary alive without us. . . . You never would have gone there in the first place."

"Maybe not." Gundhalinu shifted his weight against the hard edge of the desk. "It's a question without an answer, SB. Just like the question of what sort of justice you really deserve. I know what the law would say. But I also know . . ." He looked down at the blood drying on his palm. He raised his head again. "I know that no one comes out of World's End unchanged. The only harm you've really done is to me. And I'm not the one to judge you." He stared through them at the wall. "I've made some arrangements." He felt more than saw them stiffen. "Our family holdings are being returned—to me." "*Little enough to ask,*" they had told him; not knowing. . . . "By the time you get back to Kharemough you'll have a home to go back to. You'll have a sufficient annual allowance to let you live very comfortably. It will be supervised by someone else, of course."

"Thank you, BZ. It's more than we deserve. . . . We'll . . . we'll . . ." HK fumbled with the fastening of his coveralls.

SB said nothing. Gundhalinu pushed away from the desk. "Get up, SB. I never said you could sit down."

He watched his brother rise from the chair. SB stared at him for a long moment, and then nodded, imperceptibly; his mouth pulled back in a sardonic smile. "I guess you have changed."

"I'll take that as a compliment." Gundhalinu folded his arms, holding his side. "If either of you ever attempts to alter the arrangements I've set up, you'll both be stripped of all class rights and completely disinherited. If either of you ever attempts to profit further from the discovery of the stardrive—if either of you ever makes public any claim at all—I'll have you on trial for charges you never even dreamed of." He pointed toward the desk terminal. "I'll be following you to Kharemough, soon enough. Your records will always be on file, wherever I go. Don't ever think I won't be able to find you. Or that I'll ever forget what you did to me."

SB glared. "That's blackmail."

"I prefer to think of it as the spirit of the law, as opposed to the letter." Gundhalinu shrugged. He turned, reaching across his desk to summon the guard. The door to the office opened, and a patrolman entered. "You have your orders?"

The patrolman nodded.

"And you have yours." He looked at his brothers for the last time. And then he turned his back on them, staring out at the rain until they were gone.

When he turned back again, he was almost disappointed that he did not find the ghost of his father waiting. Fire Lake had only made his ghosts visible; they had been real, and he had been living with them, all of his life.

He sat down in his seat again, propping his head in his hands. "Well, there, Father, it's done. Have I laid you to rest at last?" The silvery music of the antique watch filled his ears. He looked up; he shook his head slowly, leaning back in the chair.

He held the watch in his hand. *The past is always with us; even if it's in ruins.* He sighed. He had obeyed his father's final wish, and the taste in his mouth was gall. His father had been weak, rigid . . . human. Not any kind of a god. The act itself was as meaningless to him now as the value system that made it necessary. He looked down at his wrists. The smooth brown skin still bore a faint pinkish cast left by the cosmetic surgery. He touched his forehead, another scar smoothed over, and pushed restlessly to his feet.

The window was waiting for him, covered with tears. He went to it, and pressed his throbbing hand against its cold comfort. Looking out, he saw the Pantheon illuminated by a rare shaft of late-afternoon sun. He wondered whether the crowds would take it for an omen.

Meaningless—the ceremony tonight, all the rest of it; only the ornaments of vanity disguising the naked body of the truth: an overeducated madman with a death wish had stumbled on the secret of Fire Lake. *They say it takes one to know one.* He shook his head.

He had changed everything by unraveling the secret of the Lake, by giving the stardrive back to the Hegemony. In the weeks since it had happened he had barely had time to realize how much.

But he had had enough time to realize the obvious—that not all the changes would be good ones. Kharemough already dominated the Hegemony, and it would be Kharemough that had the technology to fully exploit the stardrive. He knew that his homeworld ruled benignly, sharing its power with the rest of the Hegemony's worlds, only because interstellar distances forced it to. Once Kharemough had had New Empire dreams . . . the Prime Minister and his Assembly still traveled from world to world, a harmless reminder of that past. How long would it take before Kharemough, with its technocratic and human arrogance, remembered those dreams and began to turn its new starships into warships?

No time at all. He had heard enough high officials on the force discussing the possibilities with the Hegemony's onplanet representatives already. And discussing the water of life, and a return to Tiamat. . . .

Tiamat should have been far down on anyone's list of important possibilities . . . except for the water of life. That rarity, that precious obscenity—few human beings could dream of tasting the immortality drug even once. But the ones who could afford it had enough power to make certain that it became available again. . . . Which meant that Tiamat would not have its century free from the Hegemony's interference. That Moon— *his Moon*—would not be allowed to live out her life and her reign in peace, let alone be given time to guide her people toward an independent onworld economy.

He touched the trefoil again, the dull stains at the point of each spine. The first, the only, thing he had thought of, when his brothers had asked him what he wanted most, was to return to Tiamat, to see Moon again. And he had realized then, in a moment of epiphany, that discovering the stardrive had given it to him.

When the Hegemony left Tiamat, and when they returned again, the people there called it the Change . . . a time when anything became possible. His wish would bring the Change again . . . an untimely Change, the last Change. And the end of all possibilities for the people of Tiamat.

And when he had realized that, he had known what he would be doing with the rest of his life. He would accept every undeserved honor given to him for his accidental heroism; take all of the prestige and influence that went with them—and make them work for Tiamat. He would finish what he had begun, on that world, in himself, so many years ago. He would make himself a hero—but not to the people who were honoring him today.

And perhaps not even to the people he would be trying to save. He would see Moon again; he was sure of it now. But she would not be the woman he remembered . . . any more than he was the man she had known. Their love had been an aberration, born out of need. If he had stayed on Tiamat it would have melted away like the snow beneath the rising sun of summer. Their worlds, and their minds, had been too many light-years apart. He would have been as wrong to stay as he had been wrong to leave. . . .

Another ghost laid to rest. He grimaced. When he returned to Tiamat—and he would, someday, as soon as it was physically possible to get there—it would be for far better, and saner, reasons than to search for a thing that had never existed. Moon was a queen now, and he was a hero. And both of them were sibyls. *Sibyls aren't supposed to want power.* He thought of Song; how he had spoken those words to her, somewhere in a dream. She had wanted to be a sibyl because she had wanted power—and the power had destroyed her, just as the lore predicted. There were very few sibyls anywhere in the Hegemony in positions of real influence. And yet he had power now, and he wanted it . . . and so did Moon.

But we didn't ask for this. She had fought her own mother's treachery to become queen—and yet he knew only her belief in the guidance, the sentient will, of the sibyl machinery had made her take the throne. She had believed that the sibyl machinery manipulated circumstance and her own actions toward an end that even she might never fully understand. He wondered whether she understood it now.

He had been manipulated, too, in ways he had never expected . . . though whether it was by some hidden will or simply the hard hands of fate, he still had no idea. Had going mad made him fit to become a sibyl? . . . Or had becoming a sibyl driven him sane? Was it possible that he had not been merely a footnote, a victim of circumstance, on Tiamat after all? He would never know for certain, unless he returned to Tiamat again, and asked Moon the right questions. . . .

He smiled, then—really smiled; but his mouth made an uncertain line as he remembered her ghost reaching out to him, hazed in blue. *Laid to rest? . . . Oh, gods,* he thought, *is anything we ever do really done for the right reasons?*

He rubbed his eyes, looked out at the Pantheon—the home of all the gods—again. No one he really knew . . . no one who really knew him . . . would be there tonight. The people waiting there thought he was a hero. They thought he was brave, and brilliant, and honorable . . . they wanted to give him everything. They praised his modesty. *If they only knew.* His mouth turned down. But they never would—they'd never want to. They needed to believe that virtue was rewarded, that evil was punished, that order reigned. That it all had a point.

And so did he. Once he had needed to believe it so much that it had driven him insane. . . . Until he had nearly died of his own guilt, never accepting that there were some things beyond anyone's control. No one had the secret formula that would get him through a day, let alone a lifetime. Order and chaos maintained at best a fragile truce, and the universe hung in their balance. Someday, some millions of years from now, all the stars would flow out of the night sky into darkness. And then the hand of fate would turn the hourglass upside down, and they would all tumble back again. . . . Or maybe not. *If I died today, what would anyone make of my life?* He could live his life a day at a time, now, because he knew that in the end it was no one's life but his own. And because even if it all came to nothing, at least he had made a knowing choice to act on the side of order.

The first thing he would do was oversee the scientific expedition that was already forming to study Fire Lake. They would need his unique and curious expertise, for a while. At least in that role he would not be a fraud. And at least he would be able to see that Song was taken care of. He had already arranged for Hahn to join the expedition, and to take Song with her. There would be a need for sibyls there for a long time, until the Lake was back where it belonged in starships, and at peace again. He owed Song that much, he supposed, even if it was no real answer for either of them. . . . His mind turned away from the memory of her face, which could have been his own. He would have to see her face again, soon enough—see it over and over, until it was only another face.

After he was certain that suitable progress was being made at the Lake, he would go on to Kharemough. He would work to solidify his new position, gaining influence, making himself an indispensable part of the new interstellar technology. He would keep his police commandership, too, and build his power base from there. Whatever it took, whatever was needed. . . .

He looked back again for a moment into the life that had brought him to this place, considered the ordeals that had prepared him for this future he had chosen, even as they had made it inevitable. They had seemed to him like the end of everything . . . and yet he had survived them all. None of them had been more than a prelude, a moment in time that had allowed him to begin the rest of his life.

There would be no more self-inflicted wounds, no more hesitation, no more blind allegiance to rules made by human beings as imperfect as himself. He would survive anything that got in his way, because he knew he could. He would return to Tiamat, and together with Moon he would see that power passed into the right hands. Together they would start another future, they would set right old wrongs, they would— He caught himself smiling again like a lovestruck fool. He sighed. *No . . . never for the right reasons.*

His intercom bleeped loudly in the silence. "Inspector?"

He turned back from the window, startled. His sudden movement swept the antique watch from the windowsill onto the floor. His heel came down before he could stop it, crushing the gold case, the jeweled animal faces, the fragile works within.

He lifted his foot, crouched down, picking up the pieces as

gently as though he were lifting an injured child. He placed the watch on the sill again, and stood over it, looking down. His mouth trembled.

"Inspector Gundhalinu? Sir, we ought to be leaving for the ceremony—"

He began to laugh, and went on laughing, helplessly. *What miracles we are,* he thought, *and what fools.*

About the Author

JOAN D. VINGE is the winner of two Hugo Awards, one for her novel *The Snow Queen*. She has written nearly twenty books, including her Cat novels, *Psion, Catspaw,* and *Dreamfall,* and the other Snow Queen cycle novels, *The Summer Queen* and *Tangled Up In Blue*. She has had a number of bestselling film adaptations published, including the #1 bestselling *The Return of the Jedi Storybook* and novelizations of *Cowboys & Aliens* and *47 Ronin,* among others. She lives in Arizona.